WHISTLE PIG

MICHAEL J LEAMY

Copyright © 2024 **MICHAEL J LEAMY**

All rights reserved.

ISBN: **9798333775702**

DEDICATION

This bit of scribbling is dedicated to those who have the courage to dare to do. Dare to live. Dare to love. Dare to think. Dare to speak. Dare to be surrendered to God for His use in a dark world. If that is you, reader, God bless you.

CONTENTS

Chapter One	Page 1
Chapter Two	Page 16
Chapter Three	Page 29
Chapter Four	Page 41
Chapter Five	Page 52
Chapter Six	Page 67
Chapter Seven	Page 79
Chapter Eight	Page 93
Chapter Nine	Page 107
Chapter Ten	Page 121
Chapter Eleven	Page 134
Chapter Twelve	Page 149
Chapter Thirteen	Page 163
Chapter Fourteen	Page 177
Chapter Fifteen	Page 193
Chapter Sixteen	Page 206
Chapter Seventeen	Page 220
Chapter Eighteen	Page 234
Chapter Nineteen	Page 248
Chapter Twenty	Page 258
About the Author	Page 282

ACKNOWLEDGMENTS

Beta readers boost a writer's confidence. Their comments may engender changes and fine tuning in any manuscript, as long as the author is willing to listen. An outside look often sees what the writer, immersed in the work, cannot see, or is too enamored with his own creativity to accurately evaluate. Thanks to my wife, Lynda, for her tireless proofreading, going chapter by chapter as the story developed. Thanks to Brianna, Justina and Brittany for being willing to tackle the whole thing at once. The author trusts that their efforts will make this novel a more enjoyable experience for those who read it.

The author confesses he sometimes eavesdrops on conversations, and takes notes for later use. There have been those who talked of the antics of their ancestors, skinny-dipping in local ponds and sloughs in mixed groups, with no regard as to the bodies of the swimmers. Ah, the innocence of childhood! This story starts there.

PROLOGUE

Chaos and uncertainty blanketed the states east of the mountains in the aftermath of the Civil War. Union or Confederate, former combatants headed toward the setting sun, hoping to escape the horrors of a war that pitted friend against friend, brother against brother. Early clashes had been deemed a lark. Shiloh changed that perception. It has been said that after Shiloh, nobody smiled.

Those who headed westward brought with them the wounds of war, whether physical or mental. Some would heal. Others would not. Some would succumb to the wounds of the body. Hatred would drive others to continue the conflict, killing or maiming those still considered enemies. Hand-me-down hatred would ensnare and emotionally cripple those who had never seen a battlefield. 1880 saw the birth of two who would escape the burden. One would carry the message of reconciliation across the continent, a message to a divided people, a message of reconciliation to God and to each other. Those two children would grow up. But would they grow apart?

WHISTLE PIG

CHAPTER ONE

Thin fog shrouded the meadow and broke the light of the rising sun into divergent rays as it found its way through and around the lone old oak that separated the dugout home from the necessary. The misty air that had cooled the night held little promise that it would continue that chore much beyond the dawning. By ten o'clock, the fog would be burned away, and the hot path would cause bare feet to dance quickly.

"Virginia! Git yonder and do yer stuff and git back here!"

Ginny Garrett stood gazing at the pencils of sunlight that found their way through the foliage of the tree, and delighted in their gossamer beauty as floating diamond dust danced in the sunbeams. The chill made her shiver in the flour sack garment that served as her night dress and day dress. It was her only bit of clothing. Except for that drapery, the nakedness of her feet reached all the way up her eight-year-old frame.

"Ginny! Git a-goin' a-fore I help you along!" Her mother's voice sounded muffled as it came from the door that sagged when it was opened.

"I'm a-goin', Ma. I was just a-lookin' at the purdies." Ginny's bare feet padded silently down the path. She rounded the old oak, and the motion startled the ground squirrels down by the boulder patch. They stood upright at the mouths of their burrows, and called their shrill warnings: "Chink-um! Chink-um!"

In a perfect imitation, Ginny returned the call. The squirrels relaxed. They dropped to all fours, and resumed their foraging for their breakfast. The creatures of the meadow and the willow thicket around the pond were Ginny's friends. She knew and could return their chirps and chatters. She often chattered to herself in their varied languages.

In the necessary, Ginny took her pitch from the droning flies, then launched into a melodic humming of a tune of her own design as she watched a spider spinning a web in the quarter-moon cutout in the door.

"Well, Mister Spider, them there flies will multiply faster than you kin eat 'em!" Ginny's learning was more from nature than from the one-room school house on the knoll across the meadow, and the Ozarks still shaped her speech. Pa had brought Ma and Ginny west after the Cause had failed, but poverty and the entrenched drawl kept them branded by the Stars and Bars of the recent unpleasantness, now almost a quarter century in the past. The creatures God had created were kinder than the children that gathered from the folds of the hills and the bottom lands along the streams, coming from board houses that wore coats of paint. Ginny was the only child who lived in a dugout. Like the ground squirrels, her home was a burrow in the earth. She was Ginny, but the other children called her Whistle Pig, after her squirrel friends by the boulders. Toby didn't.

Toby Mason lived on the hill beyond the pond in the willows. His home was on the top of the hill, a board house with white paint and green shutters beside each window. The door did not sag. Cows grazed on the hillside below the house. Each morning, Ginny's rooster and Toby's had a crowing contest. On school mornings, Toby followed the path across the pasture. He would climb the stile over the pasture fence, and disappear behind the willows that bordered the pond. His path merged with Ginny's, and once, when they met at the merging, Toby slowed his determined pace to walk beside her.

Daisies bordered the path from the necessary, and as she padded up toward the house, Ginny gathered a handful, then added a foxglove for color. At the door, she called, "I'm a-gonna take some flowers up the hill, Ma. I'll be back in three shakes."

Her mother's voice called softly, "You do that, Honey-child, and say a prayer while you be up there. I'll fix us somethin' to git us a-goin' today."

There was no path to the fresh mound on

the slope above the house in the ground. Pa's passing had been too recent. Ginny stopped by the boulder at the end of the mound and added her wildflowers to the growing pile of withered stems and blossoms. She traced the letters etched on the stone: Edward Garrett. He had survived the battlefields, fled to escape the images that haunted his mind, labored to provide what home he could for his wife and daughter, and then died in his sleep. He had carried the horror of Shiloh with him in his mind and in his body.

"God, I ain't knowin' how come Pa had to up and die. Things shore went better when he was here to fix and do. I know Ma ain't right well, an' they ain't much money left in the pouch. Preacher John was a-talkin' about the blessin's what be ourn, but Ma an' me ain't a-gittin' so much. Cain't You do sumpin' to help us along? I'm a-thankin' You fer what we got, what with a roof and a bite, but Ma is a-worryin' away. We-uns ain't got no idea what to do. Pa usta sing about hidin' in the cleft of the rock while he dug us a home. We shore need a place to hide from all this trouble. Cain't You shelter us some? Amen."

As she knelt beside Pa's grave, the song that echoed in her mind sprang to her lips:

Rock of ages, cleft for me

Let me hide myself in Thee.

Let the water and the blood

From Thy wounded side which flowed

Be of sin a double cure

Save from wrath, and make me pure.

Though youthful, the voice that cascaded down to her mother's ears held promise of beauty that would come with maturity. Through tears, her prayer was a plea for her girl. "Oh, God, I'm a-comin' home. I beg you to save my little girl. Carry her through that dark valley I see a-comin' soon. Draw her to love my Jesus. An' I pray You bring her someone who will treasure her on this pilgrim way. Pa's gone, and I won't be here to learn her the things that she'll need to know to live fer you. Give her a hunger fer the truth of Yer Word, and someone to feed her spirit. An' hide us both in the cleft of the Rock that is our Jesus. I pray this fer His sake and Yer glory. Amen"

Hoof-beats sounded on the hill above the grave. Willie Frost's old mare topped the rise.

"Howdy, Ginny. Visiting your pa this morning?" He swung his old frame down to the ground. "Getting a little stiff, Ginny. I brought a bag of grits for you and your ma. I got a bag of carrots, and a bag of taters, and some peas and beans and salt. I got a big sack of jerked venison from Walking Eagle. Your ma can make a good stew with the stuff."

"How come he's Walking Eagle?"

"Well, Ginny, he would tell you, 'People

gone. Nest gone. Eagle not fly.' I'll head back home. You can take these bags down one at a time. Howdy your ma."

Ginny lifted one bag and headed down the hill. Her bare feet bore her silently down to the hovel in the hillside, but her humming the hymn announced her coming. She left the sagging door open for more light in the room. When she had carried all of the supplies to the house, she asked, "Ma, God does love us, don't He? Preacher John said He does, but it don't seem like it."

"Honey, He shore does. His Word says so, and He don't lie. His love is allus a-lookin' out fer our best, even when it don't seem like it. We want all our blessin's now, and some of 'em won't be ourn till later. You be jest a sprout now, and you want to be all growed up. That's a-goin' to take years. He's a-goin' to grow you and change you to make you ready fer the blessin's what He's stored up fer you. Now, you redd up yer bed, and git some vittles in you."

It was Saturday. Ginny's late breakfast of corn meal mush and one boiled egg quieted her anxious tummy. She fetched a pail of water from the pump and washed the dishes. She set the plates and cups upside down on the table to be ready for suppertime.

Following their daily routine, Ginny pulled a chair over to the open door and reached for the well-worn Bible. "What do I read today, Ma?"

"Well, I heerd you a-singin' on the hill. Whyn't you read from the tenth of John? Yer pa loved that part about Him a-hidin' we-uns in the shelter of His hand, and God a-clappin' His hand over the top. I'm a-thinkin' you start about verse 27 or so."

Ginny thumbed through the pages, stained by years of handling. "I found it. There's a buttercup pressed a-tween the pages."

"You'll find a plenty of those in that Bible. Them's markin' what yer pa called his golden promises. Read it, Child."

Ginny ran her finger down the page, read silently, then out loud:

"My sheep hear my voice, and I know them, and they follow me: And I give unto them eternal life; and they shall never perish, neither shall any man pluck them out of my hand. My Father, which gave them me, is greater than all; and no man is able to pluck them out of my Father's hand. I and my Father are one."

"There you be, Ginny." Ma brushed a tear from her eye. "His love fer you goes on an' on. The path where the Good Shepherd is a-leadin' His lambs has twists an' turns, an' you cain't allus see what's a-comin' next. But He's a-holdin' you in His hand, and God Almighty has His hand over you like a lid. You cain't be in no safer place. Trust Him, even when you cain't see whar yer headed. He knows. Let Him lead. Jest keep on a-follerin'."

Ginny squinched up her nose. "I was a-thinkin' on paths. The one to the necessary don't go nowhere else. Just there and back. There ain't no path to the...the...rock on the hill. Leastwise, not yet. The path to the school house don't seem to lead nowhere, but others jine in with it. Is schoolin' worth it?"

Ma held out her arms for her girl. Ginny crossed the room and was gathered into a rare embrace. "You cain't git too much learnin', Ginny. Learn all you kin. That's the only way you will ever git out of this here hole in the ground. I never got much learnin' when I was a sprout. Learn all you kin."

After a pause, Ma added, "There's one more path that needs a mite of trompin'. We-uns ain't bin a-walkin' over to the church since yer pa died. I'm a-thinkin' I bin a bit mad at God. We're a-goin' tomorrow. Git along down to the pond and git yer bath. Warsh yer dress, and hang it on a bush to dry, so it don't git wrinkled. Take yer time. I'm a-gonna git me a bit of a nap while yer down yonder. Somehow, I'm allus a bit weary these days. Even if I don't do nothin'."

"Do I take the towel?"

"No. Just sit you on a rock and let the sun dry you. When you and yer dress are dry, put it on and come on back. Don't fergit to warsh yer hair. Take yer comb along to pick out the tangles. Them brown curls look mighty fine if they ain't all knotted up."

^ ^ ^

Olivia Mason scowled as she shuffled through her closet. She hesitated over the dark green silk suit, then, remembering the rough benches and old chairs at the church, moved on to her creamy linen suit. She looked well enough in linen, but the silk would give a better impression. She had worn the silk in Chicago, and the linen in San Francisco. There would not be anybody from either city at the church in the valley, so she could present an elegant image without being the subject of conversation at afternoon tea in some elegant drawing room. Besides, nobody in the valley could match or surpass her linen suit. She glanced at the satin, but rejected it. It would be too warm.

"Now, I could wear these black flats, but they have soft soles. I think I'll wear my white boots instead. Those heels will give me a bit of added height, and the click of the footsteps will announce my arrival. Yes. I believe the boots will be better."

Olivia laid out her Sunday attire, and descended the stairs. She sat on the couch in the parlor, and rang the brass bell on the table. A middle-aged woman entered, wiping her hands on her apron. "Ma'am?"

"A cup of coffee, Millie. And a sweet roll. I laid out my linen suit for you to steam out any wrinkles. And tell Tobias I wish to speak with him."

Millie curtsied, and turned to go. "Yes, Ma'am. Right away."

Olivia Mason had never made the change from plebeian coffee to the more refined tea of the upper levels of society in San Francisco, but she sipped the darker beverage from fine porcelain cups. She set her coffee on the saucer on the table and swallowed as Toby entered.

"Yes, Mother?"

"Tobias, I have decided we will attend services at that church tomorrow. I wish that man would wear an ecclesiastical gown instead of that threadbare suit. But, since people in this valley seem to admire him, it is best for our reputation that we mingle with them. I would prefer that he speak less about his precious Bible, and more about the good things we can do for the community. He is certainly no Reverend Maxwell. Preacher John, indeed! Has that man no sense of dignity?

"Anyway, Millie will have your bath prepared at five o'clock. We will dine at six. Jackson can drive us around the head of the valley in the morning. We will wait so we can arrive once the others are seated. Our entrance and impression on the people there is important."

Toby stood looking at his toes. "I like Preacher John, Mother. I would call him a friend."

"That is the issue, Tobias. A man of his position should be regarded as above and aloof from the common herd. He makes no distinction."

"But he loves us, Mother. He senses our needs and tries to meet us where we are."

"Don't argue with me, Tobias. All he can do is quote the Bible and talk about Jesus. We need someone to speak of our goodness and leave the topics of sin and salvation out of it. We will go, just so people see us there. They will think better of us for it. Perhaps we might offer them something to which they may aspire. Something higher than their lowly daily existence."

After a pause, Toby said, "I've been going early for Missus Howard's class. You could come later with Jackson."

"I think you being there early may be beneficial. Just don't get too involved. Let the words go on past you. Yes. I think the early meeting will make us look even better. Go ahead."

"Mother, it's kinda hot today. Is it all right if I go down to the pond?"

"Tobias, say it's rather warm instead. I do not desire that you adopt the illiterate speech of those in this valley who are so far below your station. You are cut from better cloth. I do not want you to become like people such as those across the valley living like rodents in that hole in the ground. What do they call that girl? Whistle Pig, isn't it? Quite an appropriate name, I should say. Indeed, they live like pigs. Do not be like them."

"Mother, are we really better than other people?"

"Tobias, look at our home. Look at the clothes you wear. Look at theirs. That difference tells you they are beneath us."

"But Mother, what if none of us had any clothes? Wouldn't we be all the same? Do clothes really make us higher or lower? Preacher John says that whatever we have or whatever we don't have, Jesus died to save us all. Doesn't that make us all even?"

"Tobias, I do not need a catechism on what Preacher John says. He is only a rural preacher in a no-name church. I doubt he has a degree in theology, and certainly not a doctorate degree."

"But Mother, he knows his Bible, and he knows Jesus. He feeds his people with God's Word."

"I don't want to hear any *but Mother,* Tobias. Preacher John does not pay any attention to the realities of society, or social structure. We have more, so we are better. They have less, so they are beneath us. We notice them so people will say we have compassion. Don't talk to me about

Jesus. Jesus was an idea. Jesus is not important in society today. And yes, you may go to the pond. Just don't get your clothes dirty or wet.

"But before you go, I want to tell you some things. In two weeks, Jackson will take me to the train to Portland. There I will catch a steamer to San Francisco. Since your father died, I have business with Mister Post in California, and with Uncle George in Chicago. I will spend a month in San Francisco, and then take a train to Chicago. There I will spend the rest of the summer with Uncle George. When I return, I will know more of what lies ahead for you. I believe it is time to move you to a school that is superior to what you have here. I will be considering schools in San Francisco and in Chicago. I will look for schools that will open doors of opportunity for you, schools that will prepare you to take your place in the highest levels of society. I will also work to arrange financing for your learning, whatever you will ultimately be. Whatever it is, I want people to admire you, to look up to you. I want them to envy you."

"Did people look up to my father?"

"I believe they would have, if he had not gone off to that silly war. Imagine all of that fighting over those who do not matter in the highest ranks of society! He was in one of the most respectable professions. He had no way to go but upward.

"When he came back from the war, he was weak and wounded. He could never return to his calling, to his work. He came back an idealist."

Toby wondered what an idealist was, but did not ask. Instead, he asked, "Did he ever talk about Jesus? Did he love Him?"

His mother gave an exasperated sigh. "Yes, Tobias, he did. That's almost all he talked about. He said that after the battle of Shiloh, he lay wounded on the battlefield. There were thousands of dead and wounded, he said. Some wounded rebel heard him crying for water, and crawled over to him and shared his canteen. 'In Jesus' name', he said. He asked if your father knew Jesus, and he said he did not. I don't remember the man's name. He did not ask what color your father's uniform was. He just lay there in the dark and talked. I suppose that was when your father found religion.

"When I met him, he wanted to know if I loved Jesus. There were not many young men left alive after the war, so in order to get him to marry me, I pretended that I did. You were born five years later. That's when I told him I did not want to hear any more about this Jesus. He provided for us, but after that, he seemed to give up. So now I am free to raise you for social success. Remember who you are."

Toby scowled. "Did my father have a Bible?"

"He did. I know it is around here somewhere. I have a chest of his things in the attic. If you want to look, I'll get you the key."

"I think I'd like it. I could carry it to the

church. Not everybody has one."

Olivia Mason smiled and nodded. That Bible could be a status symbol that elevated her son in the eyes of the crowd.

For Toby, his mother's revelations were an inspiration. Jesus had changed his father. Jesus could lift the poorest sinner from the miry clay. And, if He could lift the poorest sinner, He could lift the richest sinner. Even his mother.

As Toby rose to leave, his mother said, "Tobias, lay out your clothes for tomorrow, so that Millie can steam them. Then go on down to the pond. I have some letters to write and some planning to do for the summer. Remember, though, your bath will be ready at five o'clock."

WHISTLE PIG

CHAPTER TWO

Ginny heard splashing as she ducked under the willow branches, picking her way through the tunnel that led to the shore of the pond. Water swirled around her ankles before she stepped clear of the saplings that lined the margin of the pond. She scrambled up onto the flat boulder that served as a bathing platform. The water on the other side of the stone was waist deep. Across the end of the pond was another boulder. Looking at it, Ginny saw a pile of clothes. At the far end of the pond, she saw a head and slashing arms as the swimmer turned and knifed back the length of the pond. Near the other boulder, Toby stood and flung water from his face and hair. Turning, he saw Ginny on her boulder.

"Hi, Ginny. It certainly is warm today, isn't it?"

Ginny looked at Toby with amazement. "Kin you learn me to do that?"

"What, swim? I can teach you, but you would have to be in the water."

Ginny thought a bit, then said, "I gotta warsh my dress for church tomorrow, then I'll come." She peeled off the garment, sat on the edge of the boulder and sopped and scrubbed until the stains were faded as much as they would ever be. Scrambling to her feet, she looped the straps over two willows. Water dribbling from the fabric slowed to a drip. Turning, she sat, then slid off the boulder into the water. She squealed as it swirled around her tummy. "That's kinda cold!"

Toby laughed. "You'll get used to it. Wade over here."

Ginny giggled as she looked down at her feet. The water made her legs look short, and angled them away from her. She glanced at Toby, and her foot caught against a rock. She stumbled, and grabbed wildly for Toby's arm. He caught her before she fell headlong.

"Careful, Ginny. The water makes things look different when we look at them from up above. Look by that rock that almost tripped you. There goes a crayfish walking away from it."

Ginny looked. "We allus called them things crawdads. Are they crayfish?"

"That's what people here call them. I guess they are the same thing, but they go by different names depending on where you are."

"Kin you learn me to swim like you did?"

Toby thought a moment, then said, "Can

you hold your breath and put your face in the water? Bend forward, put your hands on your knees, and dunk your face. Count to twenty before you stand up again."

Ginny tried. She bent and dunked her face up to her ears, but popped right back up. "How kin you do that? It gives me the wobblies."

Toby dunked his face and counted to thirty while he looked at Ginny's toes. Under water, her feet looked pale. So did his own.

Ginny tried again, but popped right back up. "I ain't useta water in my face, 'cept when I warsh it. Do I hafta?"

Toby looked at Ginny's concerned expression. "We can try the easier way first. Do this." He windmilled his arms backwards. Ginny did the same. Toby said, "Don't make fists. Fingers straight, and together. Good. Now, lie back in the water, with your face toward the sky. Look up. Let your feet come up. Relax. If you don't mind, I'll hold my hand under your back so you don't sink."

Gasping, Ginny said, "I...don't mind. Just...don't let...my face go...under the water!" Muscles tensed, Ginny was a stick in the pond.

"Relax, Ginny. I've got you. You won't sink. Now, do the windmill with your arms."

"They won't move!"

"One arm, Ginny. Move one arm above your

head. Now, down through the water until it is down by your side."

"I did it!"

"Now the other arm." He felt Ginny's muscles start to relax. The curve returned to her back. "Now do the windmill. Slow is all right. The faster you do the arms, the faster you will swim."

Ginny increased the speed of her arms, and Toby felt her start to move forward. He said, "I'm going to put my other hand on your tummy, so you don't swim away from me." He held her in place as she churned the water. "All right, stop. Stand up."

Panting, Ginny stood. "I did it! Was that swimming?"

"It would have been, if I had let you go. Now the other end. I'll hold your shoulders. Flutter your feet up and down, like this." Toby moved his arms up and down in the air. "Lie back in the water."

As Ginny leaned back, Toby caught her shoulders. "Now let your feet float up. Straighten your legs and kick like I showed you."

Ginny kicked her legs, bending her knees.

"You have to keep your knees straight, and point your toes down. And bring your bottom up. Don't sit in the water. Go slowly. Good. Now faster. And breathe." As Ginny's breathing changed to gasps, Toby lifted up on her shoulders. "Stand up, now, and then we will try both together."

When Ginny's breathing steadied, Toby said, "You should try arms and legs at the same time. Lean back, and I'll stand beside you and hold your middle." Ginny kicked and splashed.

"Breathe!" Toby had to raise his voice to be heard above the noise of the water. "Slow down. That's about right." Toby let go, and Ginny glided across the pond. He waded beside her, then caught her hand and pulled her upright. "You did it! You swam across the end of the pond!"

Ginny looked up and saw her dress hanging on the willows. "How'd I git back on my side?"

Toby laughed. "I let go of you, and you swam across. Now turn around. Jump up as you lean back, and do your arms and legs again. I'll stop you before you hit my boulder."

Ginny crossed to Toby's rock, and turned and swam back to her own. "I did it! But you were on your tummy when you did it. When kin I try that?"

Toby smiled. "You need to get better on your back before you try it on your tummy. You will have to learn to breathe. It's different."

"I kin practice when I come to warsh fer goin' to church. Ma says we-uns are a-goin' to go more come Sundays. I'll git my bath on Saturday, and swim."

Toby's face showed his concern. "Only practice between these two boulders, where your feet reach the bottom of the pond. Don't go out in the middle. It gets so deep your feet can't touch if you get in trouble. I'll come on Saturdays to help you until you get better. You have to get stronger so you can swim farther."

The two climbed out on their separate boulders, and sat in the sun to dry. They hugged their knees, and talked across the water.

"Toby, kin you learn me to talk good? I don't sound like other folks."

"I could teach you, Ginny. But you could teach yourself. You speak the way you do because you copied people you heard. Your ma and pa talked, and you copied them. If you listen to yourself, you talk like your ma. I know you have a good ear. I've heard you copy the ground squirrels."

Ginny sounded the squirrels' warning cry. "Chink-um! Chink-um!"

Above the pond, a squirrel replied.

Toby laughed. "See? Just like that. If you want to speak like the people around here, listen to them. Copy them. Let them teach you. I'll help you, but let your ears help you. Just don't copy everyone. You'll end up saying things you shouldn't. Don't copy the others at school. You can copy Miss Peters. Just not the other students. And don't let them hear you copying them. Copy quietly, or after you get away from them. If they hear you copying what they say, they might think you are mocking them."

"Mocking?"

"Laughing at them."

"Oh. I wouldn't be a-doin' that."

"I wouldn't be doing that."

"Doin'."

"Doing."

"Do-ing."

"That's better. Words like that say -ing, not -in. And it's doing, not a-doing."

Ginny reached down and started picking tiny gravel from between her toes. "What if I fergit?"

"Forget, you mean. It took you years to start speaking the way you do. It might take years to change that. Just keep your ears open, and even if you just think it, copy what you hear. Then say it out loud later."

"For-get. You're a'gonna have to be correctin'...correct-ing me bunches."

Toby laughed. "Going to, not a-gonna. I'm going to have to be correcting you a lot. Just don't get mad at me, Ginny. You asked."

"I did ask. I won't get mad." Ginny watched

as Toby started to get dressed. As he stepped into his shorts, she asked, "Whats them?"

"What are these?"

"What you're a-puttin'...what you're putting on."

"My underpants, you mean?"

"How come you call them that?"

Puzzled, Toby said, "Because they go under my pants, I suppose."

Ginny reached for her dress, and pulled it on over her head, then began pulling her comb through her hair.

Toby asked, "Don't you wear anything under your dress?"

Ginny shook her head. "No. I ain't got nothing like what you're a-puttin' on."

Toby's concern showed in his face. "But what if your dress comes up? Wouldn't everybody see your bottom? They might laugh at you."

Ginny frowned. "You saw all of me when we was a-swimmin'...swimming. You didn't laugh at me."

"Well, you saw all of me, too." Toby frowned, then said, "The Bible says that when God made Adam and Eve, they were naked, but they were not ashamed. I don't mind, if you don't. When we get older, it might be different. Right now, we just swim."

Ginny smiled. "I feel safe with you. You even asked if you could touch me, and you didn't touch me where you ain't a-pose to. Ma told me them places. 'Sides, I cain't swim in my dress, can I? You don't wear nothin' swimmin'...swimming."

By this time, Toby was dressed. As he headed toward the willows, Ginny asked, "Are you a-goin'...going to the church tomorrow?"

"We'll be there. I go every Sunday. My mother said she is going. If you go early, Missus Howard has a special class for those our age. She's interesting. She knows her Bible, and you can tell that she loves children."

"I'll ask Ma about a-goin'...go-ing early. But we will go to the church. Iffen Ma cain't go, I will."

∧ ∧ ∧

Toby slipped out of the house and ran down across the pasture. He jumped across the trickle of water that wandered through the valley, and scampered up the slope to the church. He had dressed to blend in with the other children.

Louise Howard was already standing in front of the benches in the corner when Toby entered. He was not late, but he was not as early as he liked to be. He had no chance to talk with Missus Howard before her lesson. He wanted to ask her some questions that had formed in his mind after what his mother had said. She said she had pretended that she loved Jesus. That troubled him.

Halfway through Missus Howard's lesson, Toby glanced around the little group and spotted Ginny in the back. He turned back to face Louise and smiled. But Missus Howard looked troubled. She kept looking back at Ginny. Toby saw tears in her eyes. He prayed, "God, Missus Howard looks sad. I think it has something to do with Ginny. Maybe You could give her a chance to get to know Ginny, and maybe talk to her about Jesus." He added a longer petition for his mother and her salvation. He saw Louise turn to look at the rough cross, and when she turned back, he kept his eyes on it.

Toby was surprised when Missus Howard sent the children out early. He saw Ginny hurry out and head for home. He did not join the general dash to the woods behind the church. Instead, he slowed his steps and walked with Timothy Hawkins. Timmy lived across the road that cut around the head of the valley. A wagon had run over his foot, and the steel-rimmed wheel had crushed the bones. Timmy could not run, and limped when he walked. He was always left behind.

"How's the foot today, Timmy?" Toby always asked Timmy the same question. He always got the same answer.

"Oh, 'bout the same. I tolerate it. It won't ever be any better." Timmy smiled. "Thanks for staying with me, Toby. The others don't mean to ignore me. I just can't keep up."

Toby nodded. "Do you love Jesus, Timmy? Remember when He healed that lame man?"

Timmy nodded. "Yes, but He's not doing that same thing now. Missus Howard said He will make me all new when I see Him in glory."

Toby laughed. "Right! You hobble around down here, but the Bible says you will jump for joy when you see Him!"

The two boys crossed the road, and among the trees, they sat on a fallen log, listening to voices up the slope. Toby said, "I saw Ginny Garrett here today. Her mother decided they should be coming to church, but I guess she couldn't come today. Ginny was alone. Her mother loves Jesus, but Ginny says she does not know Him. We should pray for her. I'm going to keep talking to her about Him."

Timmy nodded. "I'll pray, too. I'm not so close to her as a friend. You talk, and I'll pray. Jesus can save her."

Across the valley, Toby saw the buggy leave his house. Jackson was bringing Mother to church. He wished she was coming because she knew and loved Jesus, but she had said so many things that told him that she didn't that it saddened him. They had the only buggy in the valley. It had arrived after one of his mother's trips to San Francisco. Mister Post had sent it.

To Timmy he said, "Mother is coming to church today. She said she wants to be seen here. She said it improves her image. But she said she only pretended to love Jesus. Pray for her, too."

Timmy looked down at his injured foot. "My parents don't even pretend. I wouldn't even be here except for Preacher John and Missus Howard. They loved me here and loved me to Jesus."

Toby nodded. "Me, too. They can do that, can't they?"

The bell called them to hear Preacher John. Toby saw Ginny running back to the church. The two boys made it across the road before the others, running down the hill, thundered past them. The buggy passed above them, and Toby's mother made her grand entrance before the boys reached the front door. Toby whispered to his mother, "I'm going to sit in the back with Missus Howard, if that is all right with you." When she nodded, he went to the back row and wedged himself between Louise and Ginny.

In the buggy on the way home after services, Toby's mother said, "Tobias, I think that made a good impression when you condescended to sit beside that ragged girl. I just wish you had worn your suit, to present a greater contrast. However, as it is, I do believe the people took note of the superiority of station. Image and impression, Tobias. That is everything. You want those people to think well of you. However, a word of advice. When you are among them, tilt your head a bit toward the ceiling. Show your superiority. Look down on them."

Toby frowned. "But Mother, I'm not better than they are. They are God's children, and I am a child of God. Jesus saved each one of us, so we are equal."

"Nonsense, Tobias. You and I are better because of who we are in this world and because of all we have. We must keep up that distinction of rank."

"Is that why you are going to be gone this summer?"

"In part. If all goes well, I will arrange for a better education for you, as I mentioned last night. Whether it will be San Francisco or Chicago remains to be determined. My purpose, or part of it, will be to prepare you for the highest position in society. That will not leave room for all that talk about Jesus. If Jesus was a real person…" Her voice trailed away, and she left the sentence unfinished.

Toby was silent as the buggy rattled the rest of the way to the house on the hill.

WHISTLE PIG

CHAPTER THREE

The next Sunday, Louise Howard's motherly heart reached out and hugged the little girl who sat in the corner of the church and listened carefully to the Bible teaching. Her eyes again took in the thin and faded flour sacking dress. Tears sprang to her eyes, and the convicting Word came to her mind: "**But whoso hath this world's good, and seeth his brother have need, and shutteth up his bowels of compassion from him, how dwelleth the love of God in him?**"

Louise Howard turned from her flock of little lambs, and again gazed through blurry eyes at the crude cross that hung at the front of the room. Conviction wrung her spiritual core. Garrett. That was Ginny Garrett. Why had she never called on her mother? Ruthie. That was the name she had heard. That thin dress screamed "Poverty!" Yet Ginny sat with hungry eyes that revealed a hungry spirit.

Prompted from within, Louise dismissed her flock five minutes early. They walked solemnly until they reached the door of the church, and then as usual there was a general stampede outside and around to the back of the building. Ginny still sat in the corner.

Louise Howard prayed as she lowered her bulky frame onto the bench beside the girl who so wrung her heart. "You're Ginny Garrett, aren't you?"

The girl nodded.

"May I give you a hug, Ginny?"

Ginny stood up. "I 'spect so. Toby says you like us younguns."

Louise gathered the girl in her arms, and pulled her onto her lap. She carefully pulled the hem of the faded dress down as far toward the bony knees as it would reach. "I do, Ginny. Fact is, I love you, just like Jesus loves you. You know that, don't you?"

Ginny sighed, relaxing into the embrace. "Ma says He does. But I don't know Him. How can He? Iffen He does, He gots a funny way of a-showin' it. Show-ing it. Toby says I should say it that way. Pa died. He's in the ground a-hind the house. An' Ma allows she ain't long fer this world. Is that how Jesus loves me?"

Louise drew a shuddering breath. How could this desperate need have been here in her neighborhood, and she had ignored it? She clung more tightly to the girl on her lap. With her face buried in the brown curls, she murmured, "Father, forgive me. Please open the eyes of my spirit so I can see the harvest around me."

Preacher John entered from the door at the back of the platform, looking much like a dandelion that had gone to seed. White hair and whiskers framed his kind face. "And who are you holding, Lou? Find a stray lamb?"

Louise nodded. "This is Ginny Garrett. She lives on the hillside above the pond, across from the Masons."

Preacher John winked at Ginny. "Is she the one the other children call Whistle Pig?"

A frown puckered Ginny's face. She gave a soft warning "Chink-um!"

Preacher John raised one eyebrow. He uttered a soft "Chink-um!" Smiling, he said, "All right, Honey. I've been warned. I won't say that again!"

Ginny's face cleared. "You know them, too?"

Preacher John nodded. "I've had those whistle pigs as friends since I was your age. How old are you, Ginny?"

"I was eight on my last birthday. A month ago."

"Well, I've been learning from those little squirrels since I was eight. They can teach you a lot of things, like who you can trust, and when to hide, and how to be watchful. They stand up and keep an eye on things. When something is wrong, they warn each other. The Word says we are to do the same thing. **'See then that ye walk circumspectly, not as fools, but as wise, redeeming the time, because the days are evil.'** Those squirrels are always watching all around. They teach us things, now, don't they?"

Ginny nodded solemnly. "I kin trust Toby. He's...good and kind. I cain't trust Willard Stone. He leads everyone wrong."

Preacher John nodded. "He will keep right on leading everyone wrong until Jesus gets His arms around that rascal. Jesus already holds Toby Mason in His arms. Toby won't lead you where you should not go. How about you? Is Jesus holding you, Ginny?"

Ginny snuggled down in Louise Howard's arms. "I don't know as He does. I don't know Him. I ain't never seen Him."

"Take a lesson from the squirrels, Ginny. Look around. You will see Him in the faces and actions of the people who are His. God's Spirit lives in those who love Jesus. The Bible tells us how we see Jesus in others. It says, **'Howbeit when he, the Spirit of truth, is come, he will guide you into all truth: for he shall not speak of himself; but whatsoever he shall hear, that shall he speak: and he will shew you things to come. He shall glorify me: for he shall receive of mine, and shall shew it unto you.'** So watch, Ginny. It is through His own that He will draw you to Himself, and hold you when you need to be held.

Listen to His Word. I just might talk about you this morning."

Ginny's eyes opened wide, and concern lined her face.

Preacher John winked at her. "I won't mention your name, Honey. Just be sure to listen when I talk." He disappeared through the door at the front of the room again, and then Ginny heard the clanging of the church bell as it sent its clarion summons through the valley.

Louise Howard lifted Ginny off her lap and set her on her feet beside her. She gave a quick tug to the hem of Ginny's dress. "You must be growing, Ginny. That dress is sure climbing up your legs!"

"It still hides my bottom. Ain't that what matters?"

"It does, Honey, but you be careful how you sit. And keep your knees together. Is that your best dress?"

"It's the onliest one I gots."

Pain fluttered across the face of Louise Howard. "I see. Are you here alone today?"

"No. Thet there's my ma over in the corner."

Louise Howard lurched her bulk up off the bench, and waddled across the back of the church. Smiling, she said, "Good morning. Ginny tells me you are her mother. I'm glad you could come today. That bell says we have about twenty minutes before the chairs start filling up. I'm Louise Howard. Do you mind if I sit with you?"

Ruthie Garrett welcomed the possibility that she could hide behind the larger woman. "Please do. I be Ginny's ma. We ain't bin out so much sinst her pa died. An' I ain't so well myself. I do thank you fer a-lovin' on my girl. Lord knows I fret about her, nights. Iffen I die, she ain't got nobody else. I'm a-fixin' to write to one of my husband's cousins. I'll see iffen she kin take Ginny when I'm gone."

Louise caught the sick woman's eyes and looked deeply into them. Then she said, "Ruthie...may I call you that?"

Ginny saw her mother smile. It was a sad and longing smile. "I'd be pleased if you felt you could."

"Ruthie, I'd like to come over for a visit this week. Would Thursday afternoon be all right?"

"Well, now, Missus Howard, I'm sure that would be friendly, but we ain't much fer receivin' folks. The house ain't right neat."

"Call me Lou, Ruthie. That would be friendly. And I want to see you, not your house. I have some thoughts running through my empty head. I want to share them with you and see where they might lead."

"I cain't do much with the house. I'd be

ashamed you a-seein' the mess where we-uns live. Come Saturday afternoon, an' we-uns kin meet up at my husband's grave. Ginny will be down to the pond fer her bathin' a-fore we come here to the church on next Sunday."

Louise smiled. "That will be better, I think. That way, you won't have to bother about the house, and I can talk girl stuff with you while Ginny washes up."

Family by family, the little church filled up. The youngsters from Louise Howard's early gathering slipped in from their rowdiness to sit quietly with their parents. Ginny saw Toby whisper to his mother, and when she nodded, he came to the back and sat beside her. Louise Howard reached over and tousled his hair. "I'm glad you did that, Toby!"

Ginny whispered, "Preacher John said he is a-goin'...going to talk about me this morning!" Toby raised his eyebrow, and Ginny nodded. "That's what he said." After a moment, she asked, "Is Jesus a-holdin'...is He holding you, Toby?"

Toby smiled and nodded. "He sure is!"

"An' is He a-lovin'...does He love you?"

"He does."

"How do you know? Have you ever seen Him?"

"I have. I've seen Him in the face of

Preacher John, and..."

At that moment, the man in question stepped up behind the high table, and laid his Bible on it. His opening prayer was one of thanks for what he called the gospel of God's grace. He prayed that God's Spirit would open the understanding of all of those gathered, and open the heart of anyone who did not know Jesus.

∧ ∧ ∧

With no interest in what Preacher John had prepared, Olivia let her mind wander through the past week. Minor chaos had reigned in the house on the hill. Olivia Mason was limited to two trunks for her upcoming journey. Jackson had brought them down from the attic, and Olivia had designated one for San Francisco and the other for Chicago. Millie trudged up and down the stairs, carrying the garments Olivia demanded. Dresses, suits and gowns were carefully folded and placed in one trunk or the other. Thinking, Olivia would order garments unearthed from one trunk, and either transferred to the other, or taken back upstairs as rejected for the trip.

At last, Millie rebelled. "Missus Mason, these

old legs are done climbing stairs for today. Why don't we put any you won't take in a pile, and I will take them back in the morning. If you think of something you need from upstairs, we can write it on a list."

"Limbs, Millie. Say limbs."

"All right. These old limbs. I suppose I can be a tree. To me it sounds uppity. But I'll try to remember that I have limbs instead of legs. We can leave those for chickens."

Olivia stared at the older woman, and wondered whether she was being mocked. Deciding she was, she said, "Don't be impertinent, Millie. Are we having chicken for dinner?"

"No, Ma'am. We might be close, though. I'm thinking of preparing an omelet instead. The egg, not the chicken, this time."

"You may go, Millie. I have letters to write."

From her desk, Olivia pulled stationery, pen and ink. She muttered, "I'll send the same message to both men." To Mister Post she wrote:

Your advance from last summer has sustained Tobias and me while we await the benefit from the government since my husband's death from his war wounds. However, Washington has not sent an agent to interview us, and the funds are diminished. I must impose upon your generosity yet again.

In addition, I must ask if you know of a decent school for Tobias. He is eight years old, and the school here is of an inferior nature. To prepare him for his place in society, he will need a top-notch education. Might you arrange a place for him this autumn? It would be an investment in his future, and would be repaid from his earnings once he becomes established in his field.

I will be in San Francisco this next month. Perhaps we can conclude arrangements while I am there.

Writing the same message with adjustments to Uncle George in Chicago, she added:

Tobias does not know you have deeded this house to him. We thank you for our comfortable home, which is in need of some repairs, if you could advance us a bit more to cover those. Have you found out the status of Edward's family home in Chicago? Perhaps it could be converted to cash. I will arrive in Chicago by train, and intend to spend July and August there, returning in time to settle Tobias in school in September. Your assistance in these matters will be greatly appreciated.

Olivia returned to the desk for two envelopes. She pulled them from the packet, and glared at the official envelope beneath. It bore the seal of the United States Department of War, and was addressed to Mrs. James Mason. That title combined with her husband's first name proclaimed her a widow. The wording of the paper inside was burned into her mind:

Thank you for your inquiry. The benefit you mentioned was paid to your husband five years ago. On 9 September, 1883, the receipt in the file that he signed indicates he took personal delivery of the funds in the form he requested. Our agent delivered to him the bearer bond he requested rather than the usual draft. Whoever has that bond has the use of the funds. It is the same as cash. We will have no record of where those funds are spent, or who spends them.

She had searched the desk. She had opened every file and every envelope and every packet of papers. If James had received the bond, she had not succeeded in finding it. However, Mister Post and Uncle George did not need to know that the anticipated benefit had been paid and was gone. She could leave them under the impression that it was pending. That anticipation just might open their purse strings, and refresh her supply of cash.

While the desk was opened, she pulled out the key to the trunk that held her husband's things. Tobias wanted his Bible. That thought sent her mind down another unpleasant pathway. Why did Tobias dote on that church, and such an uncouth man as Preacher John? The sooner she could get him in a proper school, the sooner she might be able to sever that attachment. A real education would show him the foolishness of belief in the Bible and all that it taught. Sin and salvation! What silly notions!

She had told Tobias she would give him the key. It would give him something to occupy his thoughts and time while she was gone. The connection with his father was still fairly fresh, and she did not wish to snap it too quickly.

Pressing the hidden catch in the desk, she raised the back panel and opened the hidden safe. The stack of cash was much smaller than it had been. Where had she spent it? She counted out money for her steamer tickets and train fare, then added two stacks for spending in San Francisco and Chicago. An extra stack represented her emergency reserve. There was none for school for Tobias. She would have to prevail upon either Post or Uncle George to cover that. Her eyes narrowed. Perhaps she could get school money from both of them.

Olivia counted out expense money for Millie. She and Tobias would have to eat something. She picked up the last stack of bills, fanned it out, and scowled at it. Shaking her head, she took a quarter of it, and added that to her spending money. Millie and Tobias could eat cheap food. She would dine in fine restaurants. The stack she returned to the safe was very thin indeed. "You silly men will have to restock the safe. And soon."

WHISTLE PIG

CHAPTER FOUR

Preacher John opened his Bible to the Gospel of Matthew. He said, "I'm going to risk embarrassing Missus Howard today. I admire the work God has called her to do with the children, and her obedient desire to do the Lord's bidding. Let's look at the eighteenth chapter of Matthew's gospel. Our Lord Jesus is talking there about His little ones." He pulled out his handkerchief. "Pardon me. I was reading the portion just now, and I can't help but weep over the loving heart of my Lord."

Preacher John turned, blew his nose, and wiped his eyes as he turned back to face his flock. "If you have a Bible, read along. If you don't, just listen to our Lord's words. **'Take heed that ye despise not one of these little ones; for I say unto you, That in heaven their angels do always behold the face of my Father which is in heaven. For the Son of man is come to save that which was lost. How think ye? If a man have an hundred sheep, and one of them be**

gone astray, doth he not leave the ninety and nine, and goeth into the mountains, and seeketh that which is gone astray? And if so be that he find it, verily I say unto you, he rejoiceth more of that sheep, than of the ninety and nine which went not astray. Even so it is not the will of your Father which is in heaven, that one of these little ones should perish.'"

Preacher John turned and pulled out his hanky again. Turning back to the flock, he said, "Forgive me, Louise. I came in this morning, and was pierced to the core with conviction over our passage. I was at Edward Garrett's burying. I have not been to call on his wife and child in all of these months. Yet there was Louise Howard, holding that little lamb in her arms, loving her to the Savior. I asked the girl if Jesus held her, and she said she didn't know that He does. She said, 'I ain't never seen Him.' But there I saw the Savior, loving her through the heart of Louise Howard, and holding her in that woman's arms. There before my eyes was Louise, rejoicing over a lost little lamb, and I had not even gone seeking her. God forgive me!"

He went on to describe the Savior searching the dangerous areas for each lost sheep. "He uses those who are His own for the work of searching. If you are His, you are His heart to love, you are His arms to embrace, you are His mouth to speak the truth of His gracious love. You are His eyes to do the seeking. He has a task for you to do. Paul wrote, **'Neither yield ye your members as instruments of unrighteousness unto sin: but**

yield yourselves unto God, as those that are alive from the dead, and your members as instruments of righteousness unto God.'

"God Himself is the wise workman. Those instruments Paul mentioned are tools for His use. Our members are to be yielded to Him for His purpose. God bless you, Louise. Let Him keep right on using you!"

All around the gathering, eyes were being wiped and noses blown at the humble account of Preacher John. On the bench at the back of the church, Louise Howard hugged Ginny while she prayed, begging the Lord to draw the girl to the Savior.

After the final Amen, the people gathered filed out. A few glanced toward the visitors in the corner. Preacher John walked slowly back to Louise Howard. Her arms were around Ruthie Garrett. He heard her say, "I'll be over Saturday afternoon."

Preacher John and Louise Howard watched as Ginny helped her mother down the two steps at the church door. They saw the difficulty that slowed her steps as she rested her hand on Ginny's shoulder as mother and daughter trudged along the side hill way that led to the hovel in the ground. Tears trickled down both faces. Under his breath, Preacher John said, "Chink-um!"

Louise Howard said, "Amen!"

Preacher John took a deep breath. As he opened his mouth to speak, Louise said, "Don't spoil it now, Brother. You didn't rob me of any blessing. What our Lord is doing, He is doing for His own glory, not ours. Leave it, now, Brother."

Ginny was late from school on Monday. Ruthie Garrett watched anxiously for any movement along the school pathway. At last she saw Ginny walking slowly, head down. The ground squirrels called, but Ginny did not answer. Ruthie stumbled along the path, and embraced her downcast girl. "Sompin' happen today, Ginny?"

Ginny mumbled, "Toby got whopped with a stick today. Then he got kept after school."

"Well, I'm shore sorry for Toby. Did he do sompin' to git it?"

Ginny broke down crying. "No! It was Willard Stone done it. He got a stick and sneaked up a-hind me and lifted up my dress, and everyone saw my bare bottom. They laughed at me, and Toby grabbed the stick and put welts on Willard everywhere he could whop him. Everyone was hollerin' an' Willard was screechin' an' Miss Peters come runnin' out and grabbed the stick and whopped Toby, right in front of everyone.

"When it was time to go home, Miss Peters said, 'Toby Mason, you stay here. The rest of you, go home. I stayed just outside the door. Miss Peters said Toby had to tell her why he done whopped Willard. Toby wouldn't say, so I done told her what Willard done.

"She was mad that I done stayed. She

allowed maybe Toby done what he thought was right, then sent him home. Then she made me pull up my dress so she could see I wasn't wearin' nothin' under it. She said, 'Virginia Garrett, don't you never come here like that agin.'"

Sore of heart, Ma Garrett stumbled to a boulder, where she sat and held Ginny. "I'm so sorry, Child. I ain't done right by you. I done busted my needle, and food was more dear than cloth. I shore shoulda made you some small clothes." She was still clinging to the weeping Ginny when Preacher John came up the path.

As he approached, he noticed neither had noted his arrival.

"Chink-um!"

Ginny regarded him with a tear-soaked face. Her sobs shattered her "Chink-um!"

Preacher John knelt before the two weepers. "Can you share your burden?"

The account was soon told in its ugliness. Rage flared in the usually calm face of Preacher John. Scrambling to his feet, he said, "You two wait here. I tote some weight around here, besides my belly. I have a few words to spill down in the school house."

With a determined stride foreign to his placid nature, an agitated Preacher John stormed down the path Ginny had followed with halting tread. At the door of the school building, he did not knock. When he threw the door open, it swung on its hinges so decidedly that it slammed into the wall. Preacher John stood, filling the open doorway, but the flood of his rage filled the room.

Startled, Miss Peters whirled and dropped her broom.

Preacher John roared, "You! How dare you heap shame on top of shame on that little girl? Poverty limits what she has to wear, but to have a trusted woman make sport of her is unconscionable. I'm here as her pastor, but where you are concerned, I am the chairman of the school committee. Come with me now, or pack your stuff and leave this valley. You have humiliated and humbled her, and now you will humbly seek her forgiveness. She and her mother are waiting. Move!"

Beads of sweat glistened on Preacher John's red face as he hastened Miss Peters up the path. After an emotional scene at the boulder, Miss Peters started slowly back toward the school.

Preacher John called after her, "Tomorrow, you will ask Toby Mason's forgiveness. The same terms apply."

Turning to Ginny, he pulled a bandanna out of his pocket. "Honey," he said, "It's a spell since you were in three-cornered pants. But this will have to do you for now." He folded the bandanna in half, corner to corner. He flipped it over her head, and pulled the ends around her waist. "Plenty of room, Girl. Ruthie, do you have any pins left from when she was tiny? Nobody needs to see what she is wearing under her dress. It's not shameful, Ginny, but it will cover you until things work out. I want you to take this week off from school. Come to the church and see me one day. Maybe Wednesday. And I want to see you at church come Sunday.

"I heard Louise Howard say she is coming to see you on Saturday, Ruthie. I will have a bit of a talk with her. Let's see what the Lord does. Bless you both, now. I'm sorry it took me so long to come over here, but I'm glad I came today."

As Preacher John headed toward the church, he looked toward the boulder patch. "Chink-um!"

Two ground squirrels stood upright, watching him. Both replied, "Chink-um!"

Behind him, he heard Ginny's soggy, "Chink-um!"

∧ ∧ ∧

Olivia Mason paced from the parlor to the window beside the front door. "There is still no sign of Tobias." She lost track of the number of times she had made that trek. Anger flushed her face.

This time, she saw Toby coming up the path. He turned to wave at someone, then climbed the stairs to the veranda. Impatience made Olivia wrench the knob and jerk the door open. "Get in here, young man." Rage clipped her words. "Where have you been?"

Toby's eyes turned to his toes. "I got in trouble at school today."

"I am ashamed of you, Tobias. A most distressing rumor reached me. It must have spread throughout the valley before you came home. I was told you behaved like a common ruffian and assaulted Willard Stone. Mildred Stone is my friend, and the Stones are of our rank in society. How dare you bludgeon her son?"

"Mother, I had to. If I am to be a true man, I must defend womanhood. That has to include girlhood. Willard got a stick and lifted up Ginny Garrett's dress and showed everybody Ginny did not have any underpants. They laughed at her bare bottom."

"Tobias, you must not mention a girl's body parts. Don't say bottom. And if that trashy girl had the audacity to go to school half dressed, she deserved to be revealed. That just shows how inferior she is. Isn't that the same worthless girl you sat with at the church?"

Toby's eyes flashed as he looked his mother in the face. "Ginny is not trash, and she is not worthless. She went to school to learn and improve, and wore the only clothes she has. She may be poor, but she is of a better character than Willard Stone!"

"Tobias, do not add slander to what you have already done. Imagine. My son taking the part of that girl, against a boy of far greater consequence. You should have congratulated him for his daring."

"Mother, it is not slander. The Stones do not have anything they can call their own. They are as poor as Ginny Garrett. They are living in another man's house, taking care of it while he is in France for ten years. Willard is wearing the clothes their son left behind, because those things won't fit when the son gets back here. And I will stand up for Ginny, or any other girl when someone like Willard Stone humiliates her. He was squealing like the pig he is, and screaming like a little girl. I just wish I could have gotten in a bunch more whacks before Miss Peters took my stick and used it on me."

"Tobias! More humiliation for me? You got spanked at school? How will I ever face the valley again?"

"You can, but only if you do not praise Willard Stone. People think I did what was right. If you take the part of the Stones, people will look down on you. They will shake their heads in pity. My father told me to always protect ladies. He said womanhood was to be honored. He said they are weaker, and a man must take their part to be a man. He said the strong must protect the weak. Otherwise, he falls short of being a real man. I told him I would. That was shortly before he died. He made me promise. I must."

Olivia frowned. That sounded just like James. Always an idealist. "Well, perhaps within your own stratum of society. I'm sure he would not include that trashy girl over there."

"You are wrong, Mother. He said that was why he went to the war. It was to take the part of the weak and downtrodden. Those were his words."

Olivia sighed. She knew her late husband well enough to know what Toby said was true. She had to get the boy out of this valley, and get him into a setting where reality would overprint idealism. That religious nonsense might work in this isolated corner of the world, but the world was so much more than this valley. That which was real and valued would be found in San Francisco and Chicago. Real manhood lay in getting ahead, in helping others get ahead. And getting ahead came with dollar signs. The real value of a man lay in his gold.

She had no answer right now. "Tobias, we will let that rest over the summer. Autumn may bring some worthwhile changes. In the meantime, I wish you would cultivate some higher relationships. At whom were you waving as you came up the path?"

"Ginny Garrett. She waited, and I walked home with her until the paths parted. Her mother was coming to meet her. She was late, and I suppose her mother was worried."

That girl, again! She changed tactics. "Tobias, I want you to wear your black suit to the church Sunday. Wear your blue shirt, and the white cravat. That outfit makes you look impressive. But don't play in the woods wearing those fine clothes. Stay inside and look dignified. Find someone equally dignified when you choose a place to sit."

"All right, Mother."

WHISTLE PIG

CHAPTER FIVE

Louise Howard trudged up the hill behind the dugout house. She carried a cloth sack in one hand, and a walking stick in the other. Panting, she paused and looked up toward the grave site. She could see Ruthie Garrett sitting on the ground beside the boulder. Five minutes later, she stood gasping beside Ginny's mother.

"Go ahead and set on the rock. Eddie won't mind." Ruthie paused, then added, "I 'spect I should think about gittin' one of them boulders up here fer me. I'm a-guessin' I'll have to get Preacher John to fetch it. I'm too puny."

Louise Howard dropped her bundle beside the rock, and used her walking stick to lower herself onto the gravestone. "Ruthie, Preacher John was by to see me this week. He told me about the mess at the school. There was no call for Miss Peters to do what she did to Ginny."

Ruthie muttered, "I done the best I could fer my girl. I busted my needle, and didn't have no cloth fer makin' small clothes. I didn't figger nobody'd be a-lookin' under her dress."

"Ruthie, the Lord nudged me with his Word even before Preacher John came to see me. Can I share some things with Ginny without offending you?"

"I'm too old and sick to let things offend me. I'm afeared I ain't got much longer with my girl. I done writ to a cousin, askin' if she might take Ginny whin I die. She ain't writ back."

"Ruthie, if anything happens, I'll take Ginny home with me until your cousin shows up. But it is something more immediate I'm here to discuss, and that is Ginny's clothes. The Lord and Preacher John reminded me of something. I had two girls myself. Martha was eight, and Edith was ten. Marty was about the same size as Ginny is now, and Edie was just a couple of years older. The sickness took them both. I still have their clothes, and nobody to wear them. Is it all right with you if I give them to Ginny? She would have some to grow up into, and some for now."

Ruthie smiled up at Louise. "We ain't proud. Pore folks cain't afford to be proud. I done growed up wearing hand-me-downs. I think three cousins wore them first, and most nigh wore them out. Ginny's only got the one dress, for day, night and Sunday. An' like you heerd, she ain't got no small clothes to cover her bottom."

Louise Howard reached into the bag she had carried up the hill, and pulled out her girls' underclothes. "When you have to choose between food and undergarments, you choose food."

Ruthie gasped. "Frillies! Lord knows I never had no frillies. My girl won't want to wear a dress over them frillies!"

Louise pulled out a tiered calico dress. "This was Marty's Sunday dress." Reaching into the bag, she pulled out a dress of light green, and one of soft gray. "These were for every day." One by one, she shook out the dresses, and held them up for inspection.

"They ain't hardly been worn!"

Tears trickled down the cheeks of Louise Howard. "No. They are almost new. We had just given them to the girls when they were taken by the sickness. I've held on, keeping them just to remember my girls. Do you know what the Lord showed me? **'But whoso hath this world's good, and seeth his brother have need, and shutteth up his bowels of compassion from him, how dwelleth the love of God in him?'** In this case, it's a girl in need. Then, Preacher John told me about Ginny's trouble at school. I saw my sin of holding on to these things when they could do me no good. Ginny can wash them in a tub of water with soap, instead of in the pond. The way she is growing now, that dress she is wearing will be a shirt."

Next out of the bag came two night dresses, one of cotton and one of warm flannel. Those were followed by a pair of soft leather boots, and three pairs of socks. "I don't know if these will fit Ginny's feet. She likely has gone barefooted most of the time. If they don't, try these." She pulled out a pair of beaded moccasins. "These will stretch a bit both directions. Marty loved them..." Through tears, Louise said, "Give them to your girl with my blessing. Just look at me. I sure can't wear them!"

Hugging the dresses with one arm, and fingering the soft leather of the moccasins, it was Ruthie's turn to weep.

Splashing and laughter sounded from the pond. "Where's Ginny?"

"She's a-gittin' her bath for church tomorrow. Sounds like she's a-havin' a good time of it."

"Can she swim? That pond is a bit deep in the middle. I know. We used to swim in it when I was a youngster."

"I ain't a-thinkin' she kin swim none. I told her to stay in the water where she can stand on the bottom and have almost half of her a-stickin' out. She said there is a big rock at one end, and it ain't too deep there." Ruthie started putting the dresses and other clothes back in the bag.

Louise put the under garments on top, and said, "The clothes in the bottom were Edie's. They'll do for Ginny when she grows up a little. There's a chemise down there to cover her on top when she starts to grow there."

Things quieted down at the pond, and the two mothers continued their visit until the squirrels called, "Chink-um!"

Louise laughed. "Count on those whistle pigs to sound the alarm. I'll bet Ginny's coming up the path right now."

At that moment, Ginny rounded the old oak and, looking up to where her mother sat, she scampered up the slope. Breathless, she stopped at the foot of Pa's grave.

Ruthie said, "It sounded like you had a mite of fun with your bath."

Ginny giggled. "It was fun. We had a race, and I won!"

Ruthie looked puzzled. "A race? You and who else? You cain't win agin yerself!"

"It was me and Toby. Toby's bin learnin'...teaching me to swim. I won!"

"Did you swim in your dress?"

"No, Ma. We didn't wear nothin' to swim in."

"Toby didn't neither?"

"No. We just swam, then put our clothes on, and here I am."

Louise interrupted. "Ginny, why don't you take this bag down to your house, but don't look in it. Then walk slowly back up here. Don't run."

Puzzled, Ginny took the bag and started

down the hill.

When she was out of earshot, Louise said, "Don't look shocked, Ruthie. Didn't you go swimming with other children when you were a child?"

Ruthie nodded.

"Boys and girls, Ruthie?"

"Well, yes."

"Did you wear anything?"

Ruthie's face reddened. "No. We took off all our clothes and left them on a rock."

"So did I, Ruthie. We swam in that very pond. Boys and girls. All naked, and we didn't think anything of it. We swam and laughed and had a grand time. Then we got dressed and went home. Our folks did not say anything or ask any questions. They had done the same thing. Now, tell me. Did you look and see that boys were made different than girls?"

Ruthie hesitated. "No-o-o…"

Louise persisted, "And when did you stop swimming naked, Ruthie?"

Ruthie Garrett giggled. "It was whin I started to git lumpy. I didn't want none o' the boys a-lookin at me then."

"And when did you start swimming with

your friends again, Ruthie?"

"I was fourteen. But then it was only the girls went a-swimmin', and we had swimmin' dresses then."

"Here comes Ginny. Don't say anything that might make her think she has done something wrong. Tell me before she gets here. Did you and your husband ever go swimming naked in the pond?"

Blushing, Ruthie said, "We did. But it was innocent stuff in marriage."

Louise laughed. "We did, too. And for Ginny and Toby, it is the innocent stuff of childhood. Let it pass, Ruthie. Your are too close to it. Let me say a word to each of those children. Don't stir the soup before there's anything in the pot."

By this point, Ginny stopped in front of the two women. She pulled up her dress, revealing the bandanna. "Ma, did I git this thing on right?"

It was with difficulty that Louise kept a straight face. "Did Preacher John help cover you, Ginny? Run down to the house and bring that bag back up here, would you?"

Louise helped Ruthie up off the ground while Ginny pounded back up the hill. To the girl she said, "Stand between us, Ginny, and take that thing off." Pulling a frilly garment from the bag, she said, "Here, step into these, pull them up and tie the ribbon."

Ginny stood gazing at her middle. "Kin I show Toby?"

Louise laughed. "Ginny, those are girl things. You only let the boy you marry see those."

"Oh. Toby ain't said nothin' about gittin' married. I guess he cain't see these. Not yet, anyway."

Louise pulled the gray dress out of the bag. "Skin out of that dress, and slip this one over your head. Good. Now, reach behind your head and button the back of the neck. Now, stand there beside that rock and let us look at you." Ginny stepped from between the two women. "Honey, you look lovely. Your pa would be proud to look at you like that."

∧ ∧ ∧

Toby pushed through the willows on his side of the pond. He shook his head as he emerged from the foliage that screened the scene of enjoyment from the house on the hill. Indeed, the fringe of willows concealed the water from the whole valley. Toby stopped, and scowled at his home above.

To no one he muttered, "We are not better. We are not higher just because our house is up there." Clothes made no distinction once they were not worn. The pond cooled both of them equally, and the water drops glistened on both faces. He trudged halfway up the hill, and turned to watch Ginny's progress. It surprised him to see her bypass her home, and scramble up to her father's grave. It was only as she arrived that he noticed the two women there. He sighed, knowing she would not wave.

His mother awaited him on the veranda. "Tobias, I heard voices. I heard laughter and yelling. What were you doing down there?"

"I was swimming. It is quite hot today."

"But I heard more than your voice, Tobias."

"I was teaching Ginny how to swim. She goes to the pond for her bath, and it is better if she knows how to keep herself safe."

"You were swimming with that girl? But you don't have any swimming clothes. And your clothes are not wet."

Toby giggled. "We don't need clothes to swim. We took them off."

Olivia stared at her son. "You swam without clothing? With a girl?"

Toby looked puzzled. "Yes. Ginny is a fast learner. We had a race, and she won."

Olivia stomped her outrage. "Tobias, I do not approve of such behavior. Such actions are inappropriate and definitely beneath you. How shameful! How low! Why, it is vile. What in the world does that trashy girl expect to get from you? Get inside! I see those women on the hill over there. I will return."

Toby was astonished at his mother's wrath. He watched as she picked her way down the hill, stepping carefully across the streamlet. He closed the door as she started up to the gravesite.

Seeing Olivia descending the hill, Louise told Ginny, "Honey, take the things down to the house. Wait for your mother there. You will not want to hear the things that are coming our way."

Ginny was out of sight by the time Olivia arrived. She stood panting, red-faced from her unaccustomed exertion. When she caught her breath, she glared at Ruthie. "I will not have your trashy girl corrupting my son! He is not a social ladder to elevate her among her betters!"

Louise roared with laughter. "Betters, indeed, Olivia? You stormed over here for a reason?"

"That woman's daughter getting my son to swim without any clothing. Is that not reason enough? The girl is nothing but trash, just like her mother!"

Louise exploded with anger. "Olivia, shut your foul mouth! Beware! One of these days, you are going to find yourself stripped naked, and it won't be for swimming. You'll lose that cloak of phoniness you wear here. Now, go home. When you come this way again, it had better be to beg forgiveness of these poor people. Their poverty does not make them trash as much as your haughty lies do it for you. Humility would be a more suitable garment for you. Now, go!"

After church on Sunday, Olivia rose from her place of prominence, and cornered Preacher John. "I will not be here a week from next Sunday. I am leaving for the summer. I will be in San Francisco and Chicago until late August. I want to know, though, why you don't lead these people in the ways of what is real? Why do you focus on myths and fables, and paint foolish pictures of this Jesus? Life here is real. If there is an afterlife, it is not our reality. Be like the theologians in the big cities. Humanity is what counts."

"How do you know what is real, Olivia Mason?"

Olivia turned to see the stout figure of Louise Howard, fists planted firmly on her ample hips. "You come here to be seen and admired, not to admire the Savior who died to save your miserable soul. You view humanity as a seven-layer cake, and yourself as the icing, when you are not even on the platter. You view clothing and possessions as the things that divide people into social strata, and denigrate the little ones who dare to strip away those artificial walls and enjoy the companionship you shun. You are going to San

Francisco and Chicago. For what? You are going to beg for more money from those who have been financing your phony lifestyle here. I am going to pray that they refuse to give you any more.

"You are a fraud, Olivia. That mask you wear blinds you to what is real. Preacher John is genuine. You will continue to be a fake until Jesus gets His arms around you and makes you into the real person He intended you to be. Those rags of superiority you wear look cheaper than Ginny Garrett's flour sacking dress ever did. Jesus can strip those rags off of you, and clothe you in His own righteousness. Only then will you reach the level of equality with those in the body of believers. Close your mouth, Olivia. You look as silly as a gasping catfish."

Olivia Mason's face flamed. "And what makes you so knowledgeable of my affairs? You are inventing lies to besmirch my good name!"

Louise's mouth was a thin straight line. Her eyes flashed. "It may have something to do with the fact that my maiden name is Post. It might be related to the fact that George Mason manages my investments. It might be that these men wondered how you behave yourself among the poorer people in this valley. Olivia Mason, your whole life here is a lie. Ruthie Garrett and Ginny are honestly poor. They do not pretend otherwise. Those dear ones are not trash, as you call them. Try that slipper on yourself. Believe me, it will fit."

Louise Howard's voice had been brittle and

quiet as she began. Her voice had gotten louder through her tirade. Mouths and eyes around the little group were gaping. Seeing others staring, Olivia whirled toward the door. Her boots rattled a rapid tattoo across the wooden planks and down the stairs. Laughter waited until she scrambled into her waiting buggy, and her carefully matched horses started down the road toward the house on the hill.

Preacher John pulled his handkerchief from his pocket and dabbed his eyes. "I shouldn't have laughed, Lou. I really shouldn't. But, oh, my. I should have sent you to talk to Miss Peters. How long have you been saving that?"

Louise sighed. "I should have asked the Lord to set a watch before my mouth. I don't know that that was spoken in love, Preacher John. It just came over me. She called Ruthie trash, and gave the same label to Ginny. Why, you should have seen poor Ruthie wither when she heard those words. I warned Olivia the other day that someday someone was going to strip her naked of her phoniness. I just did not think it would be so soon, or that I would do it. Was I wrong, Preacher John?"

"I don't think so, Lou. Maybe it was better you at the back of the church, than me at the front. But, Lou, I'm going to join you in that prayer. I'm going to pray that the Lord will open her eyes so she can see her real need is Jesus, not money. She is such a little person."

Louise glanced downward. "And I'm large."

Preacher John sighed. "People can be little in different ways, Lou. She is little inside. She has little compassion. She has little love. She has such a hard little heart."

When Toby got home, he walked slowly into the house.

"Tobias, I am leaving next Monday morning. I hope you are satisfied. I have never in my life felt so humiliated, and it was the consequence of your action. I'll get you out of here this autumn, but you will be here this summer. I do not want you doing things with that girl. Find other friends. See if perhaps you can make amends with Willard Stone.

"Pay no attention to what that woman said at the church. She is ignorant. She only thinks she knows what she is talking about."

"Do we really live in a house that is not ours? Do we really live on money that you have to borrow?"

"Don't ask foolish questions, Tobias. I told you that woman is ignorant. We have a home, and we have money." She pulled an envelope from her bag. "Here. Take this to Millie. This money will fund your summer here. It will be your last summer here, I trust. This is for food, and anything else she will need to purchase. Now, take it to her."

Toby left, then returned. "Millie said to thank you. She said she will be careful with it."

Olivia cast about in her mind for some

distracting topic to cover the earlier comments. "What is it you think you would like to do in life? You asked if you get to choose what you study. What would you choose?"

Toby's face showed his surprise. His mother had never shown any interest in things he wanted to do. "Write stuff. Stories, and maybe books. I like making stories up in my mind. Maybe I should write some of them down. I can say them out loud, but then I forget them."

"Well, Tobias, if that is something you want to try, you should do a lot of reading. I'll see if I can find you some books to fill your summer." Olivia nodded slightly. Perhaps that would keep him away from that ragamuffin girl.

WHISTLE PIG

CHAPTER SIX

Sunday morning, Ginny Garrett was *that new girl* as she sat in the back of Louise Howard's early class. The other children glanced at her, then sat whispering while they waited for the lesson. Toby Mason looked her way, then scanned the others. Puzzled, he looked at Ginny again, then grinning, he walked over and sat beside her.

"I didn't recognize you, all done up like that."

Ginny smiled her thanks. She looked down, and wiggled her feet so he would notice the moccasins that extended up and disappeared under the hem of her dress. She whispered, "I got frillies, too, but you ain't s'pose to see those 'til we get married. Least, that's what Missus Howard said."

Toby did not say anything about getting married. Instead, he asked, "But you don't swim in them, do you?"

"Oh, no, I'll take them off to swim. You cain't see them. I'll keep them dry, and you kin turn around when I put them on agin."

Toby grinned. "You swam fast yesterday, but we have to race again. I'll win next time."

Ginny tossed her head, saying, "Maybe."

Louise Howard stood, and the class quieted. Ginny got a double lesson. Toby had said she could copy Missus Howard, so in her mind, she repeated the words and inflections she heard. Louise started with the portion Preacher John had used, about the Shepherd seeking the one lost sheep. She went to Isaiah, and read, **"All we like sheep have gone astray; we have turned every one to his own way; and the LORD hath laid on him the iniquity of us all."**

She said, "That's the problem with all of us. We want our own way, not God's way. Why, I remember my own little girls. They had hardly learned to talk, when they started demanding, 'Own self!' We want what we want. We rebel against what God says, and what He has planned for us."

With gentle words and words from the Scriptures, the seeds of her need for the Savior were sown in the thoughts of the girl in the back row, were pressed into the fertile soil of her mind, and were watered as her mother, in the opposite corner of the little church, prayed earnestly for the salvation of her child.

Ginny walked to where her mother sat. The last portion from the Bible kept repeating in her mind: **"Come unto me, all ye that labour and** are heavy laden, and I will give you rest. Take my yoke upon you, and learn of me; for I am meek and lowly in heart: and ye shall find rest unto your souls. For my yoke is easy, and my burden is light."**

Toby sat beside Ginny, but Louise Howard came over and said, "Why don't you two slide over and let me sit by my friend?" Her bulk shielded the obvious poverty Ruthie's best clothes proclaimed.

Preacher John opened his Bible, and after he prayed, he looked out over his flock. "I thank the Lord that He led some of you to respond to last week's challenging word. I know that there were those who were out on the mountain searching, reaching out for those lost lambs."

A chuckle rattled through the gathering. Somehow, the story of Preacher John's enraged visit to the school had filtered through the valley. It seemed many had heard about Ginny's embarrassment at school, and Toby's action in her defense. Many had given the new girl an approving smile as they entered, and nodded in the boy's direction.

Preacher John went on, "This morning I want to be a bit discouraging. I'll say that it is important to say things in the right way. Think of what Paul wrote in his Ephesians letter: **'But speaking the truth in love, may grow up into him in all things, which is the head, even Christ.'** I have to confess that I forgot that admonition this week. I fear I spoke the truth, but

I spoke it in anger, not in love. I spoke out of love for a little girl, but I did not speak in love to the one who got the brunt of my words. That person is not here today, which is a reminder to me of another admonition in the Bible that says **'Wherefore, my beloved brethren, let every man be swift to hear, slow to speak, slow to wrath: For the wrath of man worketh not the righteousness of God.'**

"I'll have to ask forgiveness for the way I delivered my words. The Word says we are to be aware of everything, including the impact of our words. **'See then that ye walk circumspectly, not as fools, but as wise.'** That's what that word, circumspectly, means. Oh, I'm free to speak my mind. But should I? That is the question I need to remember. Whatever we think we have to say, we have to think of the way we say it, whether it is an admonition or an invitation to receive the salvation our Lord offers. The Word tells us, **'For, brethren, ye have been called unto liberty; only use not liberty for an occasion to the flesh, but by love serve one another. But take heed lest by any means this liberty of yours become a stumblingblock to them that are weak.'** If we are not careful and watchful, that is something that we do so easily. We do or say or are something that causes somebody else to stumble. We can contribute to somebody else's sin."

Preacher John had a knack for stepping on toes in a gentle way that caused his flock to think, and to grow. He could feel the intensity of the eyes fixed upon him.

In the back row, Ginny whispered to Toby, "What's a stumbling block?"

"Remember that rock you tripped over in the pond when I caught you? It made you stumble."

Louise reached beyond Ginny, and hugged the two children. "Listen, now, you two. You'll miss something."

Preacher John went on to his main point. "We are to live in a way that won't make people doubt our words. As I said last week, we are to be tools yielded to God, tools for His use as a wise Workman who knows how to use them. We have to be careful that these hands of ours don't get in the way of the Lord using our mouth. When it said for us to walk circumspectly, our walk is our lifestyle. It is the things we do, the way we behave. It's when we are not careful that we put out stumbling blocks to trip people.

"When God's Word or His Spirit prompts to do something or say something, we can argue with Him, and insist on doing things our way instead of His way. We can act in our own wisdom instead of His. We can do things in our own strength or understanding instead of His. Or we can do as Paul said, and yield ourselves to God, and our members as implements of righteousness. But, we like our own way. Paul wrote, **'Do all things without murmurings and disputings: That ye may be blameless and harmless, the sons of God, without rebuke, in the midst of a crooked and**

perverse nation, among whom ye shine as lights in the world; Holding forth the word of life.' Be His messenger. Give His message of love in a loving way. There is plenty of darkness in this world. Let His Spirit shine His light, and let Him bring glory to Jesus."

After the final Amen, Louise turned to the two children. "Ginny, would you come here to the church and see me tomorrow afternoon? And Toby, you come see me on Wednesday. I'd talk with you today, but Preacher John made me think." She picked up her bundle, and walked slowly toward the shepherd of the small flock.

"Well, Preacher John, the Lord sure used your words to change my mind today. I was going to talk to Ginny and Toby today, but you made me think again. I'll see Ginny here tomorrow, and Toby on Wednesday."

Preacher John's face got all crinkly as he smiled. "And what have those two been up to now? They are too young to get into any real trouble."

"Well, I'll tell you. Toby has been teaching Ginny to swim in the pond."

"Naked?"

"Naked!"

Preacher John chuckled. "Remember when we were their age, Louise? There was, what, eight or ten of us did the same thing? Did any of us notice that God made girls and boys different? You girls didn't stir any fleshly desires in us boys. We just swam."

"Well, you boys weren't that exciting yourselves. But I'm going to talk to those two before they notice things. I've made some swimming clothes for them. I just have to be careful what I say. Would you pray with me about that?"

"I will, Louise. If anybody can speak the truth in love, you can."

"It's how to mention stumbling blocks that needs prayer. That Ginny is nothing but a stick. She's a blank canvas, but the Heavenly Artist is sure going to work her into a masterpiece. There isn't even a promise of the beauty of womanhood the Lord has planned for her. But, it's coming. And soon. I don't want Toby to be blindsided, and I don't want Ginny unknowingly leading his mind where it shouldn't go."

"A bunch of innocents, weren't we, Lou? Oh, for those days. But they are gone forever. Do be careful, Louise. Don't tell them too much."

"Or too little. Oh, for the Lord's wisdom! Pray, Preacher John."

∧ ∧ ∧

Olivia Mason wore silk to the church. She had pulled it from the trunk, and would return it once she got home. She noted with satisfaction that she did indeed stand out in that crowd. Louise Howard and her opinions did not count for anything. She would be a peacock among all of these mallards. She missed the incongruity of the thought.

She glanced around. Toby had worn his suit and cravat. He, too, would stand out. But where was he? She spotted him sitting beside a new girl whose dress set off her complexion and eyes quite well. Good. He had found a companion fitting for his position. The two looked well together. The brown curls looked well styled. It was not fitting, though, that they sat beside that Howard woman. At least she had the good taste to appropriate a better companion than that other girl.

Olivia turned as Preacher John took his place. Her mind was already in San Francisco as he droned on with whatever he was saying. Mister Post might prove difficult. "I may have to prod him a little. A hint here, a suggestion of consequences there. That won't be blackmail. But his emotions might turn to generosity in the end."

She did not speak to anyone as she left. She noticed Tobias standing facing the girl. He appeared to bow to her, and she seemed to curtsy in response. Yes. She would certainly do for a summer companion. She looked like a girl for whom swimming naked was not an option. She must congratulate Tobias for his good taste. Surely that girl was an aristocrat.

Toby walked part way home with Ginny. "My mother is leaving Monday. I'll be here with Millie and Jackson all summer. Then Mother is planning for me to go to school in some big city. I may not get back here for years. What about you?"

Ginny stopped where Toby would turn to go up to his house. "Ma writ to Aunty Gert. She wants me to go with her once Ma goes to glory. Auntie Gert says she is a-comin'...coming next month. She said she is a-goin'...going to stay until she ain't needed here no more. I heered Ma a-givin'...giving our ground to Preacher John and the church for a buryin' ground. I guess that means other folks will git buried up on the hill with my pa. Then Auntie Gert will take me to some big city for learnin'...learning. Schooling. Then she plans to marry me off to some rich man. I don't guess I have any say in that. But I ain't a-likin' it none. If I had any money, I could git my own schoolin' and git ready for some work I would enjoy, but I ain't got nothin'. Iffen I could learn to talk right, I could write books and stories. That's what I'd rather do."

Toby looked astonished. "That's what I want to do. I could write about living on the hill, and you could write stories about living in a dug-out, and about ground squirrels, and about swimming in the pond, and about Preacher John. Oh, just lots of things. Let's try it this summer. We can write, and

I'll fix yours to make sure the words are right.

Toby bowed, and said, "And now, Miss Garrett, we must part. I shall see you tomorrow, if it pleases you."

Ginny curtsied. "G'bye, Toby. Mister Mason, that is. It'll please me."

Toby found his mother waiting for him in the parlor. "Tobias, it pleased me that you sat with that new girl at the church today. Now that was a worthy companion for you. Well groomed and well attired, she was. Do you know who she is?"

Puzzled, Toby said, "She's Virginia."

"Now, that's a fine old name. Very aristocratic. I'm sure she comes from a good family, perhaps in business, but surely in property. I want you to spend time with her this summer. What did you say her last name is?"

"I did not say. I'll maybe tell you before you leave. We may have some of the same things we like."

"If you don't find out before I leave, you can write to me. I'll leave addresses for you. Now, I have a couple of buffalo hide grips in the attic. Please go up and bring them down. They will hold the overnight things I will need for the trip, and things I will need on the steamer or on the train. That way I won't have to bother anyone for my trunks."

"What color are they?"

"One is black, and the other is brown. That is a good thing. I will know what is in each one. They feel knobby on the outside."

When he returned, Olivia held out her hand to him. "Here, Tobias. This is the key to the oak trunk in the attic. It contains some of your father's things. You desired to look for his Bible. You have my permission to go through the contents. There may be something of interest in there. Help yourself. That key will open an inner compartment, too. There is a boxed set of pistols in the chest, but I will not give you the key to that. You do not need to play with them.

"One more word, Tobias. You know what is right and what is wrong. Do what you see as right. I will be gone by the time you come down for your morning meal. I will see you in August, and we will journey into your future."

She jumped ahead to August. "In September, I am going to try to get you into a boarding school. You will live there and study there. I believe you may have your own room, but you may have to share with one or more boys. You must be the leader, not the follower. No nonsense. I want you to be the best student in the school, with the top marks. That is what will open doors of opportunity for you once you finish."

"Will I get to choose what I want to be?"

"The first few years will be basic education.

Later, you may be able to specialize. Pick something that will make a lot of money, whether you like it or not. However, I do believe you will find either San Francisco or Chicago much more interesting and exciting than this Oregon back country. You may even meet an interesting girl with a lot of money. If you do, marry her."

"Like Virginia?"

"Virginia is a little young to have a lot of money. However, her parents might have it. But you are thinking along the right lines, Tobias."

Toby turned to hide his smile. Ginny's new clothes had blinded his mother to who she really was. His mother told him not to spend time with ragged Ginny, and then told him to spend his time with well-dressed Virginia. Did that mean he should spend his summer with Ginny only when she was not wearing the flour-sacking dress? She had said he should do what he knew was right. He closed his eyes. Jesus would love Ginny, no matter what she was wearing. He nodded. "That's what is right."

WHISTLE PIG

CHAPTER SEVEN

Louise Howard sat on the church steps, praying as she waited for Ginny. "Lord, I'm right there with David. Please set a watch before my mouth. I've come a long way since I was a little girl, and I know too much to be an innocent like her. I don't want to stir up things that shouldn't be stirred. The girl is only eight, but she needs to know a little of what lies ahead. But, how much, Lord? And how do I tell her? I need Your wisdom. And here she comes, Lord."

Ginny came running along the trace that was not yet a path. She wore her old dress, but Louise saw the flash of white frillies underneath. The girl slowed, and walked the last yards, catching her breath.

Louise held out her arms and enfolded Ginny in a gentle embrace. "What a lovely afternoon, Ginny. And what a lovely girl. You must be growing. That dress in almost a shirt, now. Your frillies are sticking out down there!"

Ginny grabbed the hem of the dress, and pulled it almost up to her shoulders. "I like my frillies. Thank you fer givin'...giv-ing them to me. They cover my bottom."

"They do, Honey. They cover you out back, and up front, too. And that's important. You are getting to be a big girl now, and you should keep your girl parts covered. That's something I wanted to talk to you about."

Ginny looked solemnly into gentle eyes. "Is that a-cause I was swimming with Toby? He didn't touch where he wasn't a-pose to."

Louise smiled, and held Ginny at arm's length. "No, Honey, Toby honors you as a girl, and he wouldn't." She gathered the girl onto her lap, and started untangling the curls that had knotted up in the night. "I was talking with your mother after your bath. We were remembering when we were your age. We used to go swimming, just like you did. I remember swimming in that very pond, with eight or ten other children, boys and girls. We were just a bunch of kids having fun. We didn't wear any clothes, either.

"But I was growing, just like you are. I told your mother I...um...started to get lumpy."

Ginny giggled. "Miss Peters is all lumpy up here in her clothes."

Louise thought, "Thank you, Lord. I'll go there." She concentrated on a particularly difficult tangle above Ginny's ear, then said, "Honey, it won't be long before you start to get lumpy there, too. I didn't want anybody to see me there, just like you don't want anybody to see your bottom. I stopped swimming with those kids. I still swam with the girls, but not with the boys.

"I found out later that the boys were changing, too, and they didn't want us girls to see them. Then when we were about twelve, somebody gave my mother some swim clothes for me. I told my girl friends, and they got some. Then the boys heard about them, and they got some for themselves. Their boy parts were covered, and our girl parts were covered, and we were all back in the pond. You won't believe this, but when I was your age, I was a skinny little thing like you are. But, Honey, we don't stay that way.

"The Bible has something to say to us girls about covering ourselves. It says, '**In like manner also, that women adorn themselves in modest apparel.**' Apparel is clothes, and modest means it covers up our girl parts."

Ginny frowned. "Miss Peters gits all buttoned up clear to her chin. Andy Phillips comes by the school to see her when it's time fer we-uns...for us to go home. When she sees him a-comin'...coming, I mean, she unbuttons clear down so her lumpy parts show. That's all he looks at. And she got mad at me a-cause I didn't have no frillies to cover my bottom."

"Ahem! Well, Ginny, some people say one thing for others, and do something else themselves. You do what the Bible says. Never mind Miss Peters."

Ginny thought for a moment, then asked, "Whin I marry Toby, kin he look at me?"

"Honey, if you marry Toby, he can look at all of you."

"If we are married, kin we go swimming in the pond without no clothes?"

"Ginny, when you are married, you and your husband can swim in the pond, with or without clothes. I'll tell you a secret. I did that with my husband. Your ma and pa did, too. In that very pond."

Ginny's eyes opened wide. "Without no clothes?"

"Yes, Honey. Your ma and I talked about that when you told her about Toby teaching you to swim. I reminded her that we swam with boys and girls when we were your age. I told her to let me talk to you. And then I did not know what to say. I didn't want to tell you too much or too little. I sure did not want to make you feel like you did something wrong.

"Now, I made you some swimming clothes. Here. Take these." She handed Ginny a bundle of clothes. "I made the short pants bright red, so you won't get lost in the pond. I made the top dark green, and loose enough that it won't keep you from using your arms. Now you scoot around back to the necessary and put them on. Don't wear your frillies under the swim pants, though. Then come on back and show me how they fit."

Ginny came back around the church holding the pants up with one hand, and carrying her dress and frillies in the other. "The pants are kinda big. If I let go, they fall down."

Louise chuckled. "Here. Let me help you. I made them a little bit on the large side for two reasons." She reached inside the waist band and pulled out the ends of a ribbon that ran through the hem. "You tie these to make the pants fit around you and stay up." As she explained, she tied the ribbon and tucked the bow and the ends inside the pants. "There. Grab the sides and try to pull them down. If you can't, that's tight enough. There's enough room that the pants should last you until you are ten or eleven."

Ginny tried. "They get stuck here by these bones."

"Good. That means they will stay up when you swim. You don't want to swim out of your pants, Honey. You are just a slip of a girl right now, but you will grow toward being a woman. That will be the time to start thinking about marrying. Now, go around back and change into your clothes. I'm going to have a talk with Toby. I want the two of you to keep swimming, but pick a time that is different from your bath time. Put on your swim clothes before you go to the pond. Then, when you are done swimming, sit on a rock wearing your swim clothes while they dry. But keep them on. It's time for you to start saving the treasure of your nakies as the special gift you will give to your husband, Honey."

Concern puckered Ginny's face. "Will Toby like my nakies whin I git bigger?"

Remembering, Louise chuckled, then rocked with laughter. "Ginny, God made boys so they are delighted with the treasures of womanhood their wife brings to them. Whoever you marry, believe me, your husband will more than like your nakies. It might be Toby. You never know. That's a few years away. Now you go change your clothes."

Wednesday afternoon, Toby jumped the spring that fed the pond, and hurried up the hill to the church. Louise Howard sat on the steps. She smiled at him, and said, "Hi, Toby! I like that shirt you are wearing. Is it new? Here, sit beside me."

The boy sat, and said, "Good afternoon, Missus Howard. No, it isn't new. It was hiding in the back of my closet. I thought this was a special time, so I wore it. You wanted to talk to me?"

"I do, Toby. First, I wanted to thank you for standing up for Ginny at school. What Willard Stone did was very wrong. I hope you whopped him a couple for me."

Toby looked down at his feet. "I feel bad about what I did. I was mad. The Bible says to be angry without sinning. I got the first part right. But did I sin?"

Louise hugged the boy. "Toby, God made you to be a man. Real manhood protects and shelters womanhood. Willard Stone is a boy, but he may never be a real man. You did what God built into you. What Willard did was sin. The Bible talks about uncovering nakedness, and condemns it. I honor you, Toby, for what you did."

"Willard says he is going to get me."

"He won't, Toby. Willard is a coward. He thought Ginny was weak and vulnerable. It's those that cowards attack. He did not know she had a noble knight as a champion. If he tries, put him down. Feel your chest. Trace that bone in the middle down to your tummy. If he tries anything, that is where you plant your fist, as hard as you can. Don't hit his face. Those bones are hard, and you'll hurt your hand more than you'll hurt his senseless head.

"I want to thank you for teaching Ginny to swim, too. That way, she will be safe in water. Are you going to keep teaching her?"

"When I can. She learns fast. She beat me in a race."

Louise laughed. "I know. I was there when she came up and told her mother. She said that you want another race!"

"I do. I'll win next time, I think. But Ginny sure can move through the water!"

"There's something about that I have to talk about, Toby. You and Ginny are both growing up. You are growing toward being a man, and she is growing toward being a woman. The Bible says something about the men who served God. It says,

'And thou shalt make them linen breeches to cover their nakedness; from the loins even unto the thighs they shall reach.' I made you these swimming pants to cover your boy parts when you and Ginny are swimming. I made some to cover her girl parts. You two will honor each other, and honor the Lord's Word that way. You are both growing up, and your nakies should be saved for your partner when you are married. You and your wife can swim in the pond without clothes when you marry. Her nakies can delight your eyes. But it's time you and Ginny cover up when you are together. That will keep your mind and thoughts pure, Toby." She held out a pair of black swim pants. "I made these a little baggy so you can wear them for a couple of years as you grow. There's a ribbon around the waist that you tie to hold them up. Keep them on, and sit on a rock in the sun to get dry.

"Another thing. Ginny gets her bath on Saturday. Why don't you do your swimming together on other days? That way, Sir Knight, you will protect her dignity and modesty."

Toby squared his shoulders. "I'll do that. For Ginny."

∧ ∧ ∧

The house on the hill was quiet. Toby dressed for the day, and wandered downstairs to the kitchen. Millie looked up from her cleaning, and said, "Well, young man, they've gone. Jackson headed for the train station an hour ago. You can sit here in the kitchen, or I can bring your meal to the dining room. Which will it be, Tobias?"

"Can't you call me Toby? Mother is away, and everybody else does. And I can eat there in the kitchen. It is more homelike. Besides, you're comfortable to be around."

"Thank you, Toby. I like that. But your mother likes to maintain the distinction of rank, as she calls it."

Toby scowled. "I know. I don't like it. There isn't any rank. Aren't we all just people?"

"You know that, Toby, and I know that. But your mother pretends she is better. What are you going to do today?"

Toby pulled the trunk key out of his pocket. "First, I'm going to the attic. My father's Bible might be in a trunk up there. I'm going to look for it. Mother gave me this funny key that is supposed to open it. Do you love Jesus, Millie? My father did. Mother doesn't, though."

"I do, Toby. I used to go to that church before your father died. But your mother feels I should not sit beside her. She told me to stay here and prepare lunch. 'The midday meal,' she called it. I sure miss Preacher John. He makes Jesus real. Would you mind if I walk with you of a Sunday? I would not want to be too uppity and have Jackson drive me in the buggy. Besides, he snorts at Jesus."

"I'll pray for Jesus to save Jackson. And I'd like you to walk with me. You could sit with me and Ginny and Missus Howard. Mother calls Ginny trash, but she is one Jesus died to save. I think it is funny. Mother told me to stay away from Ginny when she saw her in poor clothes, but then Ginny came in a new dress, and Mother thought she was a rich new girl. She told me to spend the summer with that new girl."

Millie laughed. "You do that. You pray for Jesus to gather that lamb in His arms, Toby."

After he had eaten, Toby climbed the stairs and ducked through the low door to the attic storage area under the rafters. Cobwebs veiled the small window at each end of the low-ceilinged room. In the dim light, Toby saw the oak trunk pushed back to where it touched the ceiling. He felt the leather handles at each end, and found them stiff and hardened with age. He wrestled the trunk over to the door and out into the hall.

Toby unbuckled the straps. Unoiled for so long, the lock resisted his efforts to turn the key. When it finally yielded, he lifted the lid and smelled the familiar scent of his father. For a moment he knelt there, remembering.

The tray held a heavy locked box. Toby set it aside. "That must be the pistols." In the other section of the tray, he found a sock tied with a string. He untied it, and poured out twenty gold coins, each embossed with the words, Twenty Dollars. Inside was a scrap of paper that read, "For Toby." Another yielded the same number of coins, and a paper that read, "For Millie." The socks with gold rested in a blue Union kepi. Beside the uniform hat was a bundle of papers tied with string. Toby laid those aside. He would look at them later. Maybe Preacher John could tell him what they were, and what they meant.

Under the tray, Toby found his father's uniform, a canteen, a sword and a haversack that held the Bible, which he hugged for a moment. He laid the Bible aside, along with the socks of gold. He replaced the tray and the locked box, and locked the trunk. When he had pushed it back into its storage place, he picked up his treasures and walked thoughtfully down the stairs.

In the kitchen, he said, "Millie, I found something of yours in the trunk. My father wanted you to have this." He handed her the sock of gold.

"It's kinda heavy, Toby. Are you sure it's mine?"

"I'm sure. I looked inside. Open it."

Millie's face was drawn into a frown between her brows as she untied the string, and poured gold onto the table. Surprise showed in her face. "Toby! Are you sure this is mine?"

"Reach in the sock. There's a paper in it."

Millie pulled out the paper. Tears blurred her eyes as she read, "For Millie." She wiped her eyes on her apron and said, "It is sure enough your father's writing. I remember he said he had reserved something for me. I suppose this is what he was talking about. I'll just hold on to it, and keep it for an emergency. I don't need it now."

Toby nodded. He said, "I'll take these things to my room, and read in the Bible some. Then I'll change my clothes and go down to see if Ginny is in the pond. I'm teaching her to swim. Missus Howard made us some swimming clothes. We won't swim naked any more. Missus Howard said I would guard Ginny's dignity and her...something else. Modesty, I think it was, if I wear something when we go swimming."

Millie smiled. "That is a good thing. Keep on that path, and you will grow to be a noble man, Toby. Truly noble. Your father would tell you the same thing. Not every boy grows up to be a real man."

Ginny was already swimming when Toby got down to the pond. She smiled as he waded out from the willows. "I've been practicing swimming across this end. Can we try swimming the long way today?"

"We can try it, but we won't race. It gets

deep in the middle, so I will stay with you. If you get in trouble, put your arm around my middle, and I'll swim you to where you can stand up."

The two swam the length of the pond four times. It was only on the fourth pass, as they were headed back to their boulders that Toby felt Ginny's arms grab him as she coughed and sputtered. He swam toward shore, and helped Ginny find her footing. He held on to her as she doubled over with coughing. When she caught her breath, she gasped, "I must have been too close to you. A wave went over my face as I was taking a breath."

"Sorry, Ginny. I'll try to be more careful. I have to see you so I know where you are."

Ginny looked at Toby. "I like it when you hold me." She leaned and planted a kiss on his cheek. Toby released her, and rubbed his hand across his face.

"You kin...can wipe it off, Toby, but it's too late. I put it there. Thank you for helping me. I grabbed you when I started to sink."

Toby's face showed his concern. "You started to sink? I'm glad I was with you. You'll be all right as long as we stay together."

"But you are going away. How can we stay together if you are in San Francisco or in Chicago?"

"I mean here in the pond. If we stay together when we swim. But you might go away, too. Where does your Auntie Gert live?"

"I think she lives in Portland, but she said sumpin...somethin'...something to Ma about moving to San Francisco. Wouldn't it be funny if we both lived in the same city?"

Toby smiled at Ginny's corrections. "You are listen-ing and learn-ing, Ginny. Keep correcting yourself. That way, you won't stand out, whichever city turns out to be your home."

WHISTLE PIG

CHAPTER EIGHT

The smile that had never made it to Olivia Mason's eyes slowly faded. The face of Mister Post was cold and condemning. The sick feeling in her stomach, telling her she had gone too far, matched the anguish of the *mal de mer* that had plagued her on the steamer journey from Portland. She had taken a week to languish in her lodging, recovering before meeting with Mister Post. And now, the key she had thought would open his vault had snapped.

Without raising his voice, Post said, "Please join us, Ethel."

The fashionable blonde Olivia had relegated to part of the ambiance of the hotel restaurant closed her folder, rose, and crossed to their table as Mister Post pulled another chair from a neighboring table. Her face was expressionless as she glanced at Olivia, but her eyes blazed. Once she was seated, Post resumed his chair and slowly steepled his fingers.

"Ethel, this woman is Olivia Mason, widow of her late Union husband. She lives on the fringe of the Willamette Valley south of Portland. Missus

Mason, Ethel is my accountant, my secretary, and my wife. She is my security in these encounters. You may recall seeing her in that same chair each time you came to wheedle money from me. As my secretary, she has recorded our conversations word for word. Shall I have her read back to you your veiled threat of blackmail?"

Ethel Post opened her folder. Olivia shook her head, shock and humiliation competing for dominance on her face.

Post continued, "Very well. Know this. The last time we met, I offered to put my attorney on your case, investigating the status of the war benefit you have used as collateral for my loans to you. You refused, saying you had your own attorney. I had mine investigate anyway. Do you have that report, Ethel?"

His wife shuffled through the papers in the file, and handed him a single sheet.

"My attorney interviewed the agent for the War Department who delivered the benefit to your husband. It was in the form of a bearer bond, rather than a draft. Since your husband signed the receipt, I will conclude you knew nothing of the settlement. That will absolve you of fraud. In light of that, I was prepared to cancel the debt for two advances against the benefit. I will tell you now that I have changed my mind in the light of your attempt to blackmail me."

Olivia watched as Ethel continued to write.

Post continued, "I will open an account in Salem, since that is near where you live. You will deposit fifty dollars each month into that account. When you have paid the utmost farthing, as the Word says, I will send you the transcript of today's conversation. If you miss paying, I will present the transcript in court.

"I will add that I have no interest in funding your son's education, and will not contact or attempt to influence any of the boarding schools here in the city. I am on the board of directors for one, and support three others. I would recommend refusal of any applications you might submit. You may return to the Valley and continue to pretend to be more than you are.

"But first, you will be here tomorrow at this same time. You will sign the agreement for payment. After that, you will have no direct contact with me or my wife. I will see you here tomorrow, or I will see you in court the next day."

When Ethel had finished writing, she closed the folder, and the Posts rose to leave. Olivia sat in stunned silence. Her web of deceit played through her mind. Then her eyes narrowed in cunning contemplation. There was still Uncle George. She would leave early for the trip to Chicago.

The Posts were already waiting when she entered the dining area the next day. Olivia had a carefully composed look of contrition on her face.

"Mister Post, I was very wrong in what I did

yesterday. I apologize." She laid fifty dollars on the table. "To show good faith, I would like to make the first restitution payment up front."

She noticed that Ethel had her folder open and was already writing.

Post nodded. "You understand that using that word, restitution, amounts to a confession of guilt, don't you?"

Startled, Olivia compressed her lips.

Post had torn away the mask she had donned. "I have learned to read people, Olivia Mason. You read like bad copy. Even your so-called good faith is a sham. I will take your money, and give you a receipt for the sum. Make that in duplicate, Ethel.

"I have arranged with the Salem bank to receive future payments. This is your payment for July. The next is due by the end of August. If it is not paid, you may expect a U. S. Marshall to conduct you to this city in September. Is that clear?"

Olivia gulped, closed her eyes and nodded.

"Good. Now sign the two copies of the receipt, and the two copies of the agreement. Wait." He waved the head waiter over to the table. "Sir, I need you to sign these documents as a witness, if you will."

When all of the signatures were added, he

shook hands with the waiter, slipping him a tip. "Thank you, Sir."

The waiter nodded, then stepped back into his prominent obscurity. Ethel gathered her copies into her folder, and handed Olivia her copies.

Post picked up his hat, bowed stiffly, and said, "Good day to you, Madam. This closes our dealings, unless you fail."

With those ominous words, he was gone.

Olivia gathered her papers, her mind already in Chicago. She would have to maneuver Uncle George carefully. She must not bungle that conversation as she had done with Post. She had badly misjudged his caution. She must be careful with her husband's brother. He was her last possibility of financial security.

In her room, she mindlessly stuffed garments into the San Francisco trunk. When the lid would not close, she sat on the garments to crush them into place. Then she sat on the lid, and managed to close the latch and buckle the straps. Her Chicago trunk was already checked at the railway station. This one she would ship to Portland on the northbound train, have it transferred to Salem, and notify Jackson to collect it.

Her misplaced anger at Post was generalized to San Francisco, and vented on the San Francisco trunk. The audacity of that man! To sneak an investigation behind her back! And then to accuse her of fraud! She kicked the trunk, and immediately regretted it. She hobbled to the table to write letters to Tobias and to Jackson. She would send a telegram to Uncle George.

∧ ∧ ∧

The July sun scorched the air, and perfumed it with the fragrance of drying willow leaves, but the pond stayed cool as the spring poured cold water from the depths of the earth into it. Toby and Ginny enjoyed a daily afternoon swim. Ginny had mastered the rhythm of breathing as she swam face down. Toby had insisted she lie on her tummy on a rock that lay just beneath the surface, about halfway down the pond. There, supported by the boulder, she could windmill her arms with her face in the water, breathe out bubbles, then turn and inhale under her arm as it reached ahead.

June had faded into July before Toby thought she could try it in the deeper water. He had held her in place with one hand under her, and the other on her back. When she was in rhythm, he had called, "Go!" and had released her. She had crossed the end of the pond with Toby wading beside her. He caught her before she collided with the boulder on her side.

"I did it!" In their excitement over her accomplishment, the two embraced. If Toby noticed that she kissed him lightly, he did not wipe it away.

He released her, and said, "Now swim back across. I won't help you get started this time. Jump forward so you are flat in the water, and swim. I'll walk beside you and pull you up if you get in trouble. Just swim. You can do it!"

She did. Again and again, back and forth across the shallow end of the pond, the two swam side by side, sometimes standing waist deep and giggling and splashing water on each other as they caught their breaths.

"Kin...Can we try going the long way this time?"

Toby was panting. "Lets wait. We should be rested when we try that. I'll stay close to you, but not close enough to sink you. But, if you get in trouble, grab me again. But not today. I'll walk home with you, and your clothes will be dry by the time you get there. Then I'll go back across the valley. Jackson should be back, and there might be a letter from Mother. She was trying to find a school in San Francisco to send me to in September. She said she would write and let me know, so I could start getting ready to leave." At Ginny's sad expression, he reached his arm awkwardly around her shoulders. As he pulled her against himself, she turned her head and gave him another kiss, barely touching his neck just as he stepped on a sharp rock and stumbled.

She asked, "Do you want to leave, Toby?"

"Well, the idea is a little exciting. But at the same time, it is a little bit scary. I know this valley, and I know the people here. It does not matter whether it is San Francisco or Chicago. I've never lived in a big city. Mother said I can get around on streetcars. But if the car does not go where I want to go, I have to walk. I won't know the streets. She said I would live at the school, and they would feed me. I don't know if I would stay at the school all the time, or if I would go places. I don't know if they would have church at the school. I would sure miss Preacher John."

Ginny walked in silence for a bit, then said, "Ma got a letter from Auntie Gert. She is coming, and she said she was a-takin'...taking me, I mean, and would keep me and learn...teach me to be...to be...sophisticated, I think she said. Don't that mean snooty? I don't want to be snooty. I want to write stories. She said she would keep me, and marry me to a rich man when I get older. Is sixteen older, Toby?"

"She wants to marry you to an old man when you are sixteen?"

"That's what she tole Ma. She tole Ma that she married rich old men, and then when they died, she got all their stuff. She said she don't love none of them. Just takes care of them until they die. I think that is awful. Kin...Can I love you,

Toby?"

"I guess, if you want to. I'm not an old man, though. And I'm not real rich. I did find that my father left me a sock with gold coins tied up in it. It is four hundred dollars. Does that make me rich, Ginny? But you won't get it for a long time. I'm not planning to die any time soon. I could give you one of the gold coins for an emergency. Each one says Twenty Dollars."

They had reached the old oak. Ginny looked at Toby, and said, "Promise you won't. I won't let Auntie Gert marry me to any old man. But she said if I don't do what she wants, she will turn me out. Will twenty dollars do me very long?"

"Not really. But the Bible says God will supply. Whatever He supplies will be a stewardship. That means He wants you to use it carefully, and report back to Him when you do."

Toby had two letters waiting for him when he got home, one from his mother, and the other from Uncle George. The one from his mother informed him that San Francisco was dull and boring. There were no decent schools that would have him, and that Mister Post was a miserable failure. She was leaving early for Chicago.

The letter from Uncle George left him surprised and confused. Uncle George had arranged things his mother had planned to arrange. Everything was settled before his mother arrived, and only needed his mother to sign papers.

You are my only nephew, Toby, and I have no children of my own. I have enrolled you in a boarding school. However, they will not board you until you are twelve, so I am taking you into my home as my own. You will live here and attend the school, until you are twelve. At that time, you may decide where you desire to live.

The house where you are now living belonged to my wife's brother. He went west, and he built it. When he died, we inherited it. I have deeded it to you, in trust until you are twenty-one. The house is yours. When you come here, Millie will take care of it. Your mother may live there. She may not terminate Millie, nor abuse her. If she does, she is the one who will be put out.

You, Toby, will be free to choose your own profession. Neither I nor your mother will push you into any circle or employment that does not fit. I will be your legal guardian, and none of your mother's foolish pretensions will influence your future.

I have corresponded with Henry Blackwell in Portland. He is an attorney, and will visit you to explain all of this so you will understand.

I owe this to my brother, Toby.

The letter was signed *George Mason, Chicago.*

Toby descended the stairs with a puzzled mind. The house was his own? He would live with Uncle George? He walked slowly into the kitchen.

"I got a letter from Uncle George in Chicago, Millie. I'm not sure I understand what it means."

"I got one, too. I guess I should call you Mister Toby, or Mister Tobias. My letter says I am to report to you or to Uncle George. He made me in charge of the house and land. If it needs anything, I am to let him know, and he will pay to have it done. I don't understand it all, either, Mister Toby. I thought this house belonged to your mother. At least she let on that it was hers. And all this time it was yours. Or it will be, when you turn twenty-one. I'll try to keep it nice for you. The first thing I'll tell Uncle George is that it needs a new roof and a new coat of paint."

Millie paused, then asked, "With your new position, may I still walk to the church with you? May I sit with you?"

"I'm still just Toby. I'd like that, Millie."

Sunday morning, Ginny walked slowly into the church building. Alone. Seeing Toby, she went to him, threw her arms around him, and crumpled into tears. Through sobs, she managed to say, "Ma ain't a-wakin' up never no more."

Seeing the outpouring of grief, Louise Howard dismissed the others, and gathered the two in her arms. "Lord love you, Ginny, we knew this was coming, but we did not know it would be so soon. Toby, give me the girl, and you go find Preacher John. Go hammer on that door over there."

She pulled Ginny onto her lap, crooning softly over the weeping child:

Rock of ages, cleft for me

Let me hide myself in Thee.

Let the water and the blood

From Thy wounded side which flowed

Be of sin a double cure

Save from wrath, and make me pure.

Ginny sobbed, "That was Pa's favorite hymn." The sobs that wracked the little body gradually subsided as Louise continued to hum hymn after hymn.

Preacher John stood back, waiting quietly. Louise caught his eye, and said, "Ruthie's gone to glory this morning, Preacher John. You could have come right up."

"No, Lou, that bit of time was too sacred to interrupt. What now?"

Louise said, "I told Ruthie I'd take this lamb home with me when the time came. That was a comfort to her. We discussed things. I'm going over there right now to make ready. While I'm there, I'll gather Ginny's things."

Preacher John nodded. "She asked me a month or more ago to make her a box. I have it ready. I'll get out my shovel this afternoon, and in the morning I'll fix a place for her next to Eddie. Let Millie take care of your little flock for now. I'll send a note to Gertrude tomorrow. No, I'll send a telegram. Anything I write will be twisted and rejected, but I have to let her know Ruthie is gone.

Louise left the church before the message, leaving Millie holding a child on each side of her bony frame. They were both needy, but they were both loved. "Ginny, I heard what you told Toby. But do you know what the Bible says? It says, **'As for me, I shall behold your face in righteousness; when I awake, I shall be satisfied with your likeness.'** She is already in the presence of Jesus, Ginny. Paul wrote that to be absent from the body is to be present with the Lord. Jesus said, 'I am with you always.' So if your ma is with Jesus, and Jesus is with you, your ma isn't so far away. You can't see her, and she can't see you, but she loves Jesus. Do you, Ginny?'"

"I want to. I just don't know Him. I can't see Him."

"Ginny, I love Him. I know Him. The Bible says He lives in me." She squeezed the sorrowful girl. "There. He just gave you a hug through me."

Suddenly, Ginny cried, "I DO know Him! I HAVE seen Him. He's in you, and in Missus Howard, and in Toby and in Preacher John. He's been a-lovin'...loving me through all of you and through my ma all this time. Oh, I do love Him! Now I know my ma ain't just gone! We kin put all her sickness in the ground, a-cause she said Jesus would give her a brand new body!"

"Oh, Ginny, He's been pulling you toward salvation all this time. Do you know He died to save you? Do you know He came back from death so you could have everlasting life? Do you trust Him, Ginny?"

Ginny said simply, "I believe."

Toby wriggled out of Millie's hug. He walked around to face Ginny. "Do you, Ginny?"

"I do, Toby. You showed me Jesus. Thank you."

Toby placed a hand on each of Ginny's cheeks and leaned toward her. He kissed her lips.

Ginny gasped, then sighed. "Is that a promise, Toby?"

He nodded. "It's a promise, Ginny."

WHISTLE PIG

CHAPTER NINE

The train bound for Chicago crept eastward across rolling hills dotted with sagebrush and cholla. Palo verde and an occasional saguaro reached toward the blue dome overhead. Then, the train stopped. The sun was a brazen disc that focused roasting heat on the passenger cars, turning them into ovens. Olivia Mason alternately mopped her face and fanned it. The hot air stirred by her fan was no relief from the stagnant hot air of the breezeless desert.

The conductor hurried down the aisle in her car. She flagged him down, asking, "Why are we not moving?"

"Well, Ma'am, there is a collapsed trestle ahead, and another train is piled in the arroyo. There just is no room for us on top of it." With that, he hurried on his way.

The train jerked, rattled, and started in reverse. To nobody in particular, Olivia complained, "Are we going to back up all the way to San Francisco?"

A voice behind her called, "No, Ma'am, just to the last town. Happens all the time out here. There's one hotel, and the first folks off the train get the rooms. They may have to share. The last ones off get to sleep in the church. Town folks will bring blankets. The railroad will supply food. You get jackrabbit stew and biscuits, or biscuits and jackrabbit stew, take it or leave it. That is all there is. You'll be here for about two weeks while the railroad clears the wreckage and rebuilds the trestle.

"Two weeks? I have to be in Chicago!"

Another voice rang out, "Well, lady, you git more choices there. You kin start walkin', or you kin go to the livery and rent a horse and start out ridin'. You kin rent a horse and wagon and head out drivin' where there ain't no road, or you kin be like the rest of us and shut up and wait."

"Don't be impertinent!"

"There ain't no pert meant, lady. Them's your choices. I'd take the last one, iffen I'se you."

Olivia huffed, "Well! I never!"

"Yeah, and that's the trouble with you city slickers. You ain't never. There's a lot of things you ain't never. And it's 'bout time you started. Git used to it. It might git down to a hunnert degrees long 'bout two in the mornin'."

Olivia abandoned the genteel pretense, and elbowed her way to the front of the line at the rustic hotel. The clerk was not giving any choice of rooms. She wound up sharing a bed with two women who snored. It seemed to her as if they had not bathed in weeks. The room was hot and stuffy. The three women fought over the window. Open it and let in all of the biting insects? Close it and suffocate? It was not a question of a breeze. There was none. Sharing the bed was bad, but she also had to share the chamber pot, of all things!

The prediction was accurate. It was a full two weeks before the railroad company backed another train to the other side of the arroyo, transferred all of the baggage by pack mule, and led the passengers down the rocky trail, across the arroyo, and up to the waiting train.

Once the train was rolling eastward, Olivia grumbled to herself, "Why do I start drooling whenever I see a jackrabbit take off?"

July was used up by the time the train rolled into Kansas City. As Olivia descended to the platform, she heard the announcement, "Train north to Chicago, day after tomorrow. Route your baggage before you leave the station."

The hotel in Kansas City was far more comfortable than the one in the desert. "At least I have my own room! And indoor plumbing. And a bath tub! I don't know if I will ever get the odor of those two scrubbed off of me!

After bathing, she dressed and went down to the dining room. "I wonder if they have jackrabbit stew? If they do, I'm leaving. If I never taste or smell that stew again it will be too soon!" She scanned the menu. "They even have salad!"

After dinner, she returned to her room. "Now, I must chart my course with Uncle George. Toby is first, of course. He will need to be in a boarding school. That will have to be paid by someone. Or something. The status of the family home. Then, money for me. Somehow I need to maneuver George into a corner, so he sees his obligation as my husband's brother. But I can't do whatever made Post angry. I have to make him see it is his duty. But whatever is arranged, I have to be in control."

There were no arroyos between Kansas City and Chicago, but there were sidings, and freight trains that demanded the rails. When the train finally rolled into the station in Chicago, Olivia checked in at her favorite hotel. She bathed, even though it was only mid morning, then took the streetcar to George's office. At the reception desk, she said, "Olivia Mason to see George Mason."

The receptionist waited for the word please in vain. She said, "Have a seat, if you please, and I will see if Mister Mason can see you now."

Olivia stared. "You must be new here. I will just go on back."

The receptionist stepped to block the hallway, and said, "Have a seat, Madam. You may wait here while I check with Mister Mason."

Olivia glared at the girl, then gave way. "All right. I shall wait, but be assured I shall report your impertinence to Uncle George."

The girl merely smiled. "Report away then. See what it gets you. Wait until I call you."

When she had announced Olivia was waiting, George Mason said, "Well Judy, I have been waiting for her to get here for at least two weeks. Why don't you get me a cup of coffee? Better yet, bring one for yourself. Be sure to pass through the waiting area with them. You know how I like mine. Fix yours as you like it, and we will sit here and enjoy them, and enjoy the quiet."

Half an hour later, Judy went to her desk, rummaged around for her pen and pad, then said, "Madam, Mister Mason will see you now. This way, if you please." She led the way into George Mason's office, and took a chair beside his desk. She said, "Olivia Mason to see you."

He glanced up, then said, "All right, she has seen me. Now show her out."

Olivia gasped. "I wrote to establish an appointment with you, George Mason. How dare you?"

"Oh, I can be quite daring, Olivia. What is it this time? More money?"

"George, did you get my letter? I am certain I told you what I wanted. Have you seen to those issues?"

George Mason indicated a chair. "Sit there, Olivia."

Olivia glared at Judy. "George, that girl was most impertinent to me when I arrived. I think you should let her go and employ a more congenial receptionist."

"And I think you should be more congenial with my staff, Olivia, and not presume upon relationship. Where shall we begin?"

"Is she going to stay in here listening, George?"

"She is staying, and she is listening, and she is doing anything I ask her to do. I have taken the liberty of preparing a portfolio of documents. Many will require signatures and witnesses. Judy will be one witness. I will send her for another as needed." He unwound the closure string on a packet of papers, and selected the one on top. "This document gives me guardianship of Toby Mason."

"Tobias. Call him by his name."

"I will call him by the name he chooses for himself. He is Toby. I will have sole authority to direct his affairs here in Chicago. I will oversee his education and his estate."

"George, I am his mother. Am I to have no control in his life?"

"None, Olivia. But we will return to this document later." He selected another. "You asked about the family home. It is mine, and mine alone. You have no claim to it and no interest in it. I will rent it out, and that income will finance Toby's schooling. It will not be converted to cash."

He chose a third paper. "I have chosen a good boarding school for Toby. However, the school does not board children under twelve years of age. He will therefore live in my home. He is my only nephew, and my wife and I have no children. We will keep him as if he were my own son, and once he is twelve, he can decide for himself whether he wishes to continue in our home or board at the school. It will be his choice.

"Next, the home you occupy. That home belonged to my wife's brother. When he died, it became ours. I have deeded it to Toby in trust until he is twenty-one. This paper establishes a trust for the maintenance of that home, and this paper establishes a trust for the management of the property. Millie will be in charge of that. The management trust will pay her, and you are forbidden to touch her money. In fact, you are to treat that woman with absolute respect if you wish to continue to occupy the dwelling.

"This document, Olivia, establishes a trust for you. It will pay you a set annual stipend in the first week of January. You can live comfortably and frugally on the amount. If you choose to live extravagantly, it may be used up halfway through the year. You will get no more, so don't ask. You cannot touch the principal. The stipend will be yours as long as you remain in the house. You may remain in the house as long as you desire, as long as you treat Millie with respect and dignity. Offend her, and you lose it all.

"That brings us back to the guardianship. You sign here, and I sign here. Judy, kindly call Walters to be our other witness. Walters is my attorney, Olivia. His partner in Portland is on his way even now to present these documents to Millie and Toby. Your husband had the deed to the house there, and it will be discovered and recorded before you get back to Oregon."

Olivia scowled. "This is all nonsense. What gives you the audacity to draw up all of these papers without consulting me? What if I refuse to sign this...this blackmail?"

"Funny you should mention that, Olivia. You will sign, or you lose everything. You all but demanded money, secured by nothing. You have borrowed money, citing my brother's pending war benefit. It might surprise you to discover that the Posts are our good friends. You will sign it, Olivia."

∧ ∧ ∧

Hoof-beats and the rattle of wheels announced an arrival at the house on the hill. The sound of the ornate knocker echoed through the lower level, and summoned Millie to the door. "May I help you, Sir?"

The suited gentleman handed Millie a calling card. "I'm Henry Blackwell. I am an attorney representing George Mason of Chicago. He has asked me to come here and explain some issues to Tobias Mason. Is he available?"

"Come in and have a seat in the parlor. I will summon Toby. Would you like a glass of cold lemonade? It's a warm one today."

Blackwell looked surprised. "You have ice in August? I'm amazed. But yes. Lemonade would wash down some of the dust I've managed to gather."

Millie called Toby, who came clattering down the stairs. She returned with a tray that held two glasses of lemonade. Blackwell sipped, swallowed and sighed, his eyes closed. "How in the world do you get it cold on a day like this?"

Millie laughed. "It's an old farmers trick. I wrap the pitcher in a wet towel. As the towel dries, it draws the warm out. Then I put the pitcher in a pail of spring water in the ice box. That keeps it cool on the warmest day."

Blackwell nodded. "I'd heard of that. I guess that comes from Bible times, when beads of water seeping through the clay jar evaporated and kept the water cold and refreshing in that hot climate. This is most refreshing. I thank you."

Turning to Toby, he asked, "Did you get a letter from your Uncle George? Do I call you Tobias?"

"My mother does. But everybody else calls me Toby. But yes. I got his letter."

"May I see it, Toby?"

Toby ran up the stairs, hitting every other step. When he returned, he carried not only the letter from Uncle George, but also the bundle of papers from among his father's things in the trunk. "Here's the letter, Sir, and also a bundle of papers. I found them, but I don't know what they are or what they mean. Can you tell me?"

Blackwell glanced at the letter. "Yes. This is the same as the copy I received. We will discuss some of the points." He untied the string that held the bundle of documents and unfolded the first one. "Here it is! Toby, this is the deed to the property here. It needs to be registered in Salem. We were wondering what had become of it."

Blackwell picked up a single hand-written sheet wrapped around a folded document that bore an embossed seal. He unfolded the letter and scanned it. "Oh, my!"

He grabbed the sealed document. One look at it brought forth "Oh, my goodness gracious! Toby, what do you know about the Garretts?"

Toby looked puzzled. "Well, Mister Garrett died a few months ago, and Missus Garrett just died. There's only Ginny now."

"And how old is Ginny?"

"She's eight. Like me."

"And where does Ginny live?"

"Across the pond in a dugout house. But her Auntie Gert is coming for her."

"Oh, no! Not Gertrude Garrett!" Blackwell gathered all of the papers and jumped to his feet. "Excuse me, Toby. I have to leave. I will return this afternoon. This cannot wait!"

Toby followed Blackwell to the door, and watched him clamber into the buggy. To the dozing driver, Blackwell said, "Salem. Get to the courthouse. And don't let the wheels grow any moss!" The driver walked the horses to the road, then lifted them into a ground-eating trot.

It was nearly three o'clock when Toby heard the buggy stop out front again. He opened the door before Mister Blackwell could rap the knocker.

"That was a fast trip, Mister Blackwell. Come on in. Would you like some more lemonade?"

"Thank you, Toby. You read my mind. Could I beg a glass for Simon, my driver?"

"I'll tell Millie."

"Please do, and ask her if she can stay with us. You can take Simon his lemonade. Then we can find where we were when I left so suddenly. I'll tell you what I can."

Simon had pulled the buggy into the shade under the oak trees. Both he and the horses were dozing. Simon drank the lemonade and handed Toby the glass. "Nice and cold. I thank you, Mister Toby. That was really good."

When Toby returned to the parlor, he found Blackwell and Millie finishing their conversation. "So you are in charge, Millie. If anything comes up, you tell me, and I will tell Chicago. Little things, I will just take care of them. But remember. Your money is yours. George does not want you helping Olivia carry on her false image here. If she burns through her allowance, don't give her any of yours. May I tell George you agree?"

"Please do, and thank him. Now, I'll go make some more lemonade, and get it to cooling. You can continue with Mister Toby. And when you are done, I'll have supper for you and Simon, and I'll have rooms for you redd up."

Blackwell smiled his thanks. "Now, Toby. I need to clarify a couple of points. You said Virginia Garrett's mother died?"

"It was yesterday morning, or sometime in the night. Preacher John was going to do the digging today, and then we all go for the burying tomorrow morning. Louise Howard got Missus

Garrett ready and in her box."

"And where is the girl?"

"Missus Howard took her home with her. Auntie Gert is supposed to be at the burying. Then she plans to take Ginny away."

Blackwell sighed. "Toby, I have to tell you that Gertrude Garrett is not a good woman. I had to take steps to limit what she can do. That's why I had to hurry to Salem. Now, whatever she wants, she has to ask me. I have been appointed as Virginia's legal guardian. That last paper I looked at sent me running. It was your father's war benefit paid to wounded soldiers. But it was a bearer bond. It was the same as cash. It belongs to Virginia. Read the letter your father wrote, and you will understand. If Gertrude Garrett got her hands on that bond, she would spend it on herself, and Virginia would have no reserve. I put the money in a trust at the bank. It has my name on it, and Virginia's. Gertrude cannot touch it."

After going over the points in the letter from Uncle George, Blackwell said, "I will escort you to Chicago. I have no idea why your mother is taking the long way home, but it works for us. She said she will take the southern route across the continent by train, and then catch a steamer to Portland. You and I will take the Northern Pacific or the Great Northern to Chicago. Anyway, we will go by train. I can tell you there is some marvelous scenery going that route. I've done it a few times.

"Now, Toby, where might I find Virginia Garrett? I need to talk with her, and with Missus Howard. Where do they live?"

Toby smiled. "I'm glad you are going to help Ginny. She's a poor girl."

Blackwell laughed. "Not all that poor any more, thanks to your father. Be sure you read his letter to Edward Garrett. I'm just sorry Garrett did not live to get it. Now, where is Virginia?"

Toby traced a map on the table with his finger. "You drive along the road around the head of the valley, and watch for a yellow house on the left side of the road. You will see it before you get to the church. Watch, though. It is surrounded by oak trees that shade it, but they can also hide it."

"Well, Toby, there will be two of us watching. We will find it. Tell Millie we will be back for supper. And thank you, Mister Toby, for the use of your rooms tonight. I definitely want to be at the burying tomorrow."

WHISTLE PIG

CHAPTER TEN

Olivia seethed with rage from Chicago all the way to Kansas City. Uncle George had undercut her plans at every point. She had signed the silly paper. That was the only way she would have an income, short of going to work. She was not fitted for any employment. She had no skills. "I had to turn Tobias over to that man who has no vision for all that my son could be. Let him choose, indeed! But he has money. I wish he had just given it to me. I had no idea he knew Mister Post."

That diverted her thoughts into another channel of anger. The presumption of that man! He had twisted her suggestion into blackmail, and not only refused to advance her any money, but also conveyed his notion to Uncle George. "He even sent his attorney snooping into my affairs!"

That thought sent her into a frenzy of mentally searching the house. James had signed for the war benefit, but where was it? She had looked everywhere. "It is not in the desk. It is not in the chest of drawers in our room. Did he spend it? Did he deposit it? But Post told George it was delivered."

That sent her thoughts back to Chicago, and the circle of rage started again. George had made it clear that she was a guest in her own home. "Millie, of all people. He put Millie in charge. I can't order her around. He made it clear that she is not my servant. She will be a rock in my shoe all the time. She will be a constant reminder that George has seized control of everything. Even Tobias!"

She changed trains in Kansas City, and headed west. The rhythm of the wheels on the rails drummed the circle of anger in her mind. George had her in a cage. "I need his money. I can only get money while I am in the house. I can't get rid of Millie. I will be forever trapped in that miserable valley."

Another thought intruded. "Why am I headed for San Francisco? I was not thinking when I got the ticket. That has to be the fault of George as well. He distracted me with all of his control. Now I will have to take a steamer to Portland again. I'm done with trains. At least there will be no jackrabbit stew on the steamer! The trip down was nothing but misery. This whole trip has been a worthless failure."

Such were her thoughts as the train entered the desert stretch of the journey. The rising temperature in the car raised the level of her anger. She avoided other passengers, and nursed her hurt.

The train lurched to a stop just short of the fallen trestle. Repairs were under way, but in the heat of late summer, workers labored and died under the blazing sun. Baggage was portaged to the other side of the arroyo and stacked to await the train that would finish the trip to San Francisco. The passengers had to spend the night in the cars, roasting and waiting, quarreling and complaining. Food and water would be available on the other train.

Olivia began a letter to Millie that she would post in San Francisco. She crumpled and discarded her first three attempts. Finally, she quit. She had no idea when she would arrive in Portland. "I'll wait until I get there, hole up in a hotel, and send a telegram. Choppy and short can be the fault of the method. George can't fault me for that kind of message."

Olivia did not get any sleep that night. She sat up and sweltered. A miserable night did not improve her disposition. The other train did not back into position until late the next afternoon.

She stood at the edge of the arroyo and watched the baggage being loaded. When she recognized her own trunk disappearing through the sliding door, she started down the zigzag path the other passengers had followed. At the bottom of the arroyo, she jumped back as a huge rattlesnake slithered across in front of her. She screamed as the serpent coiled itself right where the path started up to the waiting train. The conductor looked over the rim above, and called, "Get up here, lady. We won't wait all day!"

"Snake!" Olivia pointed at the coiled barrier that buzzed before her. "There's a big snake!"

Exasperated, the conductor scrambled down the steep path, picked up a large rock, and hurled it on top of the menacing rattler. Wounded, it writhed and rolled out of the way. "Now get up there and load up, lady."

Olivia took two hesitant steps, her eyes on the movements of the snake. Then she darted up the path. Panting and gasping, she climbed the steps into the car and collapsed into a seat.

At the conductor's word, the brakeman gave the signal, and the engine coughed and hissed into motion. It was seven o'clock when the train pulled to a stop at the water tower across from the rustic hotel. The conductor bellowed, "Dinner at the hotel. Jackrabbit stew and biscuits. Coffee's been burning all day. Lemonade is warm. You have one hour, and then we leave."

Over jackrabbit stew, a fellow passenger said, "It's a bad sign if a rattler crosses your path. Worse if it coils up and buzzes at you. Beware, lady."

Olivia laughed. Her laughter was tinged with nervousness. She'd already bypassed a train wreck. Another day and a half, and she should be in San Francisco. She brushed aside the superstition of the other lady.

In the city, Olivia checked into her usual hotel, then went to purchase her steamer ticket.

"Sorry, lady. The passenger steamer headed north three days ago. Won't be another until next month. However, there is a freighter leaving day after tomorrow. The *Wilma Dee*. They have staterooms for six passengers. There is one room remaining. Would you like to book it? Or, you could take the train north to Portland, and transfer to another down to Salem."

Olivia hesitated. She could not afford the hotel for a month, and definitely could not afford the restaurant. "I'll have to take it. No more trains for me. I've had enough of delays and failed tracks. I'll take the steamer." She paid the fare, and arranged for her trunk to be placed in her stateroom. She felt that the term was being stretched to cover a berth that lacked luxury. She sent a terse telegram to Uncle George: "Taking steamer *Wilma Dee* to Portland."

Back in the hotel, she went to the dining room. When she was served, she saw the Posts enter. Her dinner was suddenly tasteless.

Two days later, Olivia Mason boarded the *Wilma Dee* and opened her trunk. She laid out the clothes that would be appropriate for dining at the captain's table. She had no high expectations for the quality of the food. The crew seemed to be drawn from a variety of countries. She understood little of their conversation, and what she could make out was a badly broken English. Her nose wrinkled in disdain.

The morning the steamer was to depart, the

pumps were running. The bilge had been awash, and the keel rested on the sand. The weight of the hull pressed the propeller into the bottom of the harbor. It was only as the bilge cleared that the ship floated free.

With the mooring lines cast off, the *Wilma Dee* drifted away from the dock. The steam whistle shrieked, and she put out to sea. As the propeller brought her up to speed, an odd vibration fluttered through the hull. The white-capped bow wave curled back, forming the wake that trailed her. The wake spread, settled and vanished in the waves.

∧ ∧ ∧

Ginny stood between Henry Blackwell and Louise Howard at the graveside. Ruthie Garrett lay in the coffin Preacher John had built for her in advance. Louise had wrapped her in her quilt and placed the slight body in her final bed. Preacher John had prayed as he nailed the lid in place.

Auntie Gert trudged up the slope, and when she reached the small gathering, she glared at Blackwell. "Henry Blackwell, you are the last person I expected to see here. Why did you come?"

"I came to look after the interests of my

ward, Ginny. Why did you come, Gertrude?"

"I came to take my niece home with me. What do you mean, your ward?"

"I am her legal guardian, her defender, and the custodian of her estate. You may take her home with you. You may raise her to adulthood, but decisions as to her life and future pass through me. One thing you will not do. You will not fashion her after your own image. You told Ruthie you would marry her off to some rich old man when she is sixteen. You will not. Is that clearly understood?"

A signal from Preacher John precluded Auntie Gert's reply. Blackwell helped Ginny with her end of the rope as Ruthie was lowered. He imitated a rich, rolling Scottish burr, saying "Ginny, it's a gr-r-rand honor-r-r to tak' a rope's end at the side of the gr-r-rave o' ane ye luved." He noted that the girl was dry-eyed, while her face squinched into a puzzled frown.

Preacher John erased the frown with his words. "Ruthie is not in the box. She is finished with that body she left here. The Bible says her Savior is able to make her a body like His eternal one, free of sorrow, free of sickness, free of pain." He presented the simple gospel. Ginny smiled at Toby and nodded. She mouthed, "I believe!" Gertrude frowned and shook her head.

The people gathered stepped away after Preacher John's "Amen!" He laid aside his jacket, and said, "I brought an extra shovel, if anyone would like to help fill in."

After a moment, Louise Howard stepped forward. "I'll help, Preacher John, as long as my breath lasts. I ignored Ruthie Garrett all these years. I owe this to her. Set the pace, Preacher John. I'll match you." In an undertone, she said, "Watch those two over there. Sparks are about to fly."

Clods beat a hollow tattoo on the wooden box at the bottom of the grave. Their ominous echoing matched the ominous look on the face of Auntie Gert.

"Mistah Blackwell, how deah you intahfeah in my affay-ahs?"

"Gertrude Garrett, why don't you shed those phony feathers?"

"Gertrude Garrett, Smee-yuth, if you please."

"Oh, yes. You used that pretended southern drawl and a borrowed gown to worm your way into the life and bank account of Hiram Smith. You presented yourself as a southern belle, and enticed him into what you termed a 'marriage of companionshee-yup.' The comforts of the marriage bed were a thing of the past for Hiram, but that got you close enough to squander his wealth with your trips to Europe. He endured them, but no more."

"You, Suh, combine slander with mockery? Ah a-yum offended."

"You be offended. Just as offended as you desire. But, be careful, Gertrude. Be very careful where Ginny is concerned."

Gertrude glanced to where Ginny stood with Toby, watching the dirt fill the grave of her mother. "I've changed my mind. You keep the girl. Hiram does not want to be bothered with a child in the house. I'm going to tell him of your insolence. You will be hearing from his attorney."

Blackwell chuckled. "That's funny, Gertrude. Would you like to listen in on the conversation? 'Blackwell, Hiram Smith says Gertrude told him you were rude to her. She wants me to sue you for slander.' 'Well, Mister Blackwell, I am most ashamed of myself. But you tell Hiram I'm about to have even more to be ashamed about.'"

Blackwell's face became solemn. "Gertrude, you are misinformed. Hiram told me he is delighted to have Ginny in his home. He looks forward to having someone to dote upon and to shower with benefits. You have squandered much of his wealth, and we have taken steps to limit your access to his accounts."

Gertrude frowned. "And what do you mean by 'we'?"

"I am your husband's attorney, Gertrude."

Auntie Gert's eyes narrowed, and she pursed her lips. She suddenly saw Ginny as a rival.

Seeing the change of face, Blackwell said,

"Don't even think that way, Gertrude. It is in your best interest that Ginny stay alive and well. You have made a practice of attaching yourself to wealthy old men, and it is rumored that if they did not have sense enough to die in a timely manner, you helped them along.

"My friend, Doctor Thornton, has found ways to determine how people died, even ten or twenty years later. If anything happens to Ginny, or to Hiram, for that matter, I will open an investigation into the deaths of your former husbands. We will open their graves, and Doctor Thornton will gather his evidence. I'll be blunt, Gertrude. If anything happens to Ginny or Hiram, you will hang. Picture yourself with a cloth hood over your face and a rope around your neck as you wait for the trapdoor under your feet to drop you into everlasting fire. Close your mouth, Gertrude. You look silly with it hanging open like that.

"For the next thirteen years, I will be keeping track of Ginny's welfare. I am authorized to drop in at any time. Hiram will keep me informed. He will see to her education. He will see to her clothing. He will see to her entertainment. You will teach her the things that a mother would teach her as she grows up, unless Hiram succeeds in finding a proper governess. In that also, be very careful. My wife will interview her on those subjects. Do not poison the well. You have been warned."

On the other side of the grave, the two children stood looking at each other. Toby gave

Ginny an awkward hug. "I'm going away, Ginny. To Chicago. Mister Blackwell is taking me to my Uncle George. He lives there. I'm supposed to live with him and go to school."

Ginny nodded. "I'm a-goin'...going away, too. Auntie Gert is going to take me to her home in Portland. Mister Blackwell said Uncle Hiram wants me. Auntie Gert only wants me for what she can use me to get. But Mister Blackwell said he is my guardian and protector. He said Auntie Gert cain't...can't do nothin'...anything without either Uncle Hiram or Mister Blackwell sayin'...saying it's all right."

Toby looked down to the willows, then up to the house on the hill. "Do you think we'll remember this place, Ginny? This is the only home we have had. Will you ever come back here?"

"I want to. Will you remember your promise, Toby?"

"What did I promise?"

Ginny puckered her lips, and leaned toward Toby. "Oh, that's right." He kissed her. "I'll remember, Ginny."

"You won't marry nobody...anybody else?"

"I don't know any other girls."

"But there will be lots of girls in Chicago."

"There will be lots of boys in Portland, too."

Ginny nodded. "But I'll remember. I'm going to ask Jesus to bring us back together."

Toby stood thinking for a minute. Then he pulled a paper out of his pocket. "I'm going to pray the same thing. Chicago is a long way away from this valley." He handed the paper to her. "I want you to read this, Ginny. My father wrote it to your father. They are both dead now. But this seems to draw us together, somehow."

Ginny took the handwritten page and read, *"Dear Edward, I have finally found out who you are. After Shiloh, I lay wounded in the darkness. I had been so thirsty, and had been calling for water, again and again. There were so many of us, dead and wounded, that nobody paid any attention. Then another wounded man crawled over to me and shared his canteen. Then he asked me if I knew Jesus. He bound up my wounds as he shared Jesus with me. He was more concerned about what would happen to me if I died. Darkness hid the color of our uniforms. That did not matter any more.*

Now I discover that you, my neighbor, were that man. I can't come see you. The government has given me a war benefit for wounded soldiers. You were on the other side, so you will not get any help. I have asked that my benefit be paid as a bearer bond. I am giving you that bond, as we two are bonded together in a bond of peace in Jesus. You can spend it on a new start, or your wife Ruth can spend it, or your daughter Virginia can have it as an emergency fund to use for whatever purpose.

The war is over. There were no winners. But you and I are not enemies. This bit of money cannot pay for what you did for me, Edward, both for here and now, and for eternity. The war ended for us in the darkness of that night, but it brought the light of life. Thank you, my friend and brother."

Ginny looked at Toby in awe. She handed him the letter. "You keep this. Write a story about it. My father told your father about Jesus, and you told me about Him. Kiss me again, Toby."

He did. Then he kissed her again. Everyone started to leave. Mister Blackwell scooped Ginny up in his arms and started toward the church where the buggies waited. He called, "Say good-bye to Millie, Toby, and then come on over to the church. The train is waiting for us. You can ride with Ginny all the way from here to there!"

Toby started down the path that led past the dugout home in the hill. As he reached the bottom of the path, from the boulder patch came a chorus from the ground squirrels. "Chink-um! Chink-um!"

WHISTLE PIG

CHAPTER ELEVEN

The train ride north to Portland was a journey of wonder for Ginny, who had never traveled more than a mile from her humble dwelling. Seeing towns and farms along the tracks kept her eyes wide open with wonder.

It was shortly after noon when they rolled into the station. Blackwell gave instructions for the delivery of their baggage, then led the way to the streetcar that would take them east to Hiram Smith's estate.

Henry Blackwell escorted the two children up the stairs to the ornate door of an impressive Portland home. He pulled the cord, and the sound of a gong echoed through the house. A man in livery opened the door.

Blackwell said, "Good evening, Joseph. Is Hiram occupied? I've a surprise for him."

The butler eyed the children. "No, he is not busy right now. He's in the library. Come in, and I'll let him know you are here." Joseph Osburn led the way through the entry hall and through the parlor.

He crossed to a closed door, and rapped on it with his knuckle. A muffled voice told him to enter. He opened the door and announced, "Henry Blackwell, sir, and guests."

"Well, come on in, Henry. Who have you there?"

"This is Miss Virginia Garrett. She is Gertrude's niece. And this is Tobias Mason. He lived across the little valley from the Garretts. Virginia's mother died a few days ago, so she is an orphan. I will tell you straight out, Hiram, I went to court and was appointed her guardian. I did that to thwart the machinations of Gertrude. She told the girl's mother that she was going to raise her up and marry her off to a rich old man when she turned sixteen."

The noise Hiram made showed his disgust. "Henry, she is my wife, so I will bite my tongue. But that sound says it all."

Blackwell looked for a moment into the eyes of his friend. "Hiram, I'm taking Toby to Chicago on the Northern Pacific or the Great Northern. We will go by train, anyway. He will live with his uncle, George Mason of that city, and be educated there. By now, his mother should be returning from Chicago. When it comes to charades, she and Gertrude are a matched set. However, she met her match in the person of George Mason. George is her late husband's brother.

"When I return, there are a few things we

will need to discuss. But for now, I want Gertrude's influence to be held to a minimum. Can you manage that, my friend?"

Hiram nodded, then called, "Joseph, are you out there?"

The butler opened the door. "You called, Mister Smith?"

"I did, Joseph. Please summon Missus Pierce."

Minutes passed, and Joseph opened the door for a jolly woman, slightly plump, whose face was a map of laugh lines.

Hiram nodded, dismissing Joseph. "Henry, this is Helen Pierce. I have employed her to be a governess for Virginia."

He looked at the girl. "I am sorry, Virginia. You have been standing there, and I have not even spoken to you. You are welcome here. Do I call you Virginia? What do you call her, Tobias?"

Toby laughed. "She's Ginny. And I'm just Toby."

Hiram smiled, crow's feet crinkling the corners of his eyes. "That's friendly sounding. Ginny, this is Missus Pierce. She knows Portland, and will be your companion on outings. She will take care of your needs. Your room is next to hers. She will take care of you, and teach you." He noticed Ginny gazing at the shelves of books. "She may select books here, and read to you, or have you read to her. There is a lot of knowledge in these books, Ginny. Do you like books?"

Put on the spot by direct address, Ginny nodded shyly. "I want to write. But I gotta learn to talk right first. Toby was a-learnin'...teach-ing me."

Hiram smiled, and winked at Missus Pierce. "Listen to Missus Pierce, and imitate her. She is educated, and speaks very well, Ginny. She will teach how you should behave as you grow up. I like the timber of your voice, young lady. Can you sing?"

"I like to. I ain't sang much but hymns."

"Missus Pierce has a piano in her room. I look forward to you filling this place with pleasing music, Ginny. Helen, kindly take Ginny and show her where she will be living. Toby will be in the upstairs guest room, south suite. Then take them both, and get Toby some traveling clothes. Get Ginny something new, too. I will chat with Mister Blackwell."

When the children were gone, Hiram asked, "Did you explain the restrictions to Gertrude?"

"I did, and she did not like what I had to say. I do believe that is the reason she went directly to her apartment. Here is an interesting connection between those two children. It seems Ginny's father was a Confederate soldier who was wounded at Shiloh. Toby's father was Union, and he was also wounded there. Ginny's father saved the life of Toby's father, and James Mason gave his wounded soldier benefit to Edward Garrett. It was a bearer bond, and since both men had died, I took the liberty of placing the funds in a trust for Ginny where Gertrude cannot get her hands on the money. It is an emergency fund for Ginny."

Hiram nodded. "Good. And what about Gertrude's money?"

"I borrowed an idea from George Mason. Gertrude gets a stipend the first week of January each year. She is free to spend it as quickly or as slowly as she desires, but when it is gone, she does not get any more until the next January. Your investments are untouchable, as are your accounts. I have made every effort to safeguard your future. She cannot incur debts in your name. Those may seem like drastic measures, Hiram, but she would have left you destitute."

Hiram Smith nodded. "In the few years since I got involved in this so-called marriage, she has gone through half of my resources. I'm not all that old, Henry. I may have a good ten or fifteen years left. I have a feeling Ginny is going to bring some light into this dark home."

Blackwell paused, then said, "Hiram, it is my suspicion that Gertrude sees Ginny as a rival for your wealth. I have warned her that nothing is to happen to the girl or to you. We have discussed the rumors regarding her deceased former husbands."

Helen Pierce led the way upstairs. She

showed Toby to his guestroom, then took Ginny to her suite. "This will be your bedroom, Ginny."

Ginny saw the window, and hurried across to look out. "Missus Pierce..."

"Call me Pete, Ginny. That's quicker, and friendlier. You are Ginny, and I'm Pete. I guess it comes from Pierce. Everybody has called me Pete for years."

Looking out the window, Ginny asked, "Is the necessary in them trees, Pete?"

"The necessary? And what is that, Ginny?"

"It's where you go when you gotta go. I gotta go."

"Oh. I see. It's right across the hall, through that door."

Ginny's face showed astonishment along with her desperation. "It's in the house?"

"Come along. I'll show you."

Pete led the way and opened the door.

Ginny looked through the door, and asked, "What's them things?"

Missus Pierce laughed. "I suppose they look different than what you have known, Ginny. That thing over in the corner is called a toilet. It is where you sit. When you are finished, you pull on that chain hanging below that tank on the wall.

Just pull it and let go. Don't hold it. Try it. I'll wait outside. I'll close the door for you."

Ginny opened the door and asked, "What's that thing over there?"

Pete entered, and said, "This is where you wash your hands. Twist this knob, like this." Water gushed into the basin. "Reach in and wash your hands, Ginny. Do this each time. Now, dry your hands on this towel."

"You don't have to pump?"

"No, you just turn the knob. Then twist it the other way to turn it off."

Ginny crossed the room. "What's this big thing for?"

"That's where you take your bath. I'll get it ready for you after supper."

"I don't have to go down to the pond no more? Or wash in a bucket?"

"No, Ginny, and the water will be warm. You just undress, climb in the tub, and wash. I'll lay out a soft towel for you."

Shopping was a new experience for Ginny. She had never seen such variety. Toby was outfitted in a navy blue suit, light blue shirt with a navy blue tie and a bowler. Ginny stood beside him in a navy blue velvet dress. Both had new black shoes.

Supper was another surprise. Toby joined them in the upstairs sitting room, and the cook brought in a large tray. Instead of her usual bowl of stew, Ginny got a plate, and Pete served her a slice of ham, mashed potatoes and gravy, and green beans. There was a bowl of salad, and a plate of fruit. The variety was not new to Toby, but Ginny ate slowly, savoring each new offering. When her plate was clean, Cookie brought her tray again, and served bowls with a slice of cake awash in sliced strawberries and topped with a mound of whipped cream.

When their bowls were empty, Toby got up and said, "I'm leaving early tomorrow, Ginny. I'll be gone by the time you get up."

Ginny stood, trying to memorize the details of the boy. "You won't forget, Toby?" Her bottom lip trembled.

Pete looked from one to the other. They were only eight, but she sensed a deep bond.

Ginny squinched her eyes shut and bit her lower lip. Looking Toby in the eyes, she said, "Don't forget, Toby. Tell me you won't forget."

Toby shook his head. "I won't forget, Ginny."

"Kiss me good-bye, Toby."

Pete's eyes were blurred by tears as the two little ones kissed.

∧ ∧ ∧

Rain fell in Portland as Toby and Henry Blackwell boarded the train. Chicago was miles and days away. Hiram Smith had secured berths in a sleeping car for the two travelers. Their days would be spent in the passenger car, their meals served in the ornate dining car, and their nights in the bunks in their stateroom.

In the new suit and bowler Hiram Smith had funded, Toby looked like a miniature copy of Henry Blackwell. The conductor hid a smile as he took their tickets.

The train rolled northward, then was loaded on a ferry to cross the Columbia River to Kalama, Washington. From the river, it headed eastward into the hills. Later, Toby gazed in wonder as the train labored up the incline that led them over Stampede Pass in the Cascades, to emerge into blinding sunshine on the east side of the mountains. The first part of the journey set the pattern for the ever-changing scenery of the crossing. Mountains gave way to hills, and hills gave way to plains. The flat land was suddenly wrinkled into hills which grew into mountains. Rivers ribboned the land. Some of the streams were sullen and sluggish while others danced and frolicked on their way to the sea.

The tracks ended, and the train was taken apart, loaded on a ferry, and then reassembled on the other side of the Missouri River. Henry Blackwell was able to pull some strings, and Toby got to cross the Missouri riding at the bridge with the captain, who got a chair for Toby to stand on, and let him take the helm for part of the way.

The lonely tracks of the west gave way to a spiderweb of main lines and branch lines once they crossed the Missouri. It seemed they could choose their route, because all railroads appeared to lead to Chicago.

Once they reached that city, it seemed as if there was a station every mile. The train stopped often, and people stepped off, and then others climbed in to take their places. At the fifth stop, Henry Blackwell picked up both bags and said, "This is our stop, Toby. We take the cars from here."

"Take the cars?"

"Streetcars. They go all over the city. We will have to change cars two times. Stay with me. I think I remember all of the places and car numbers. We will get there."

They stepped down from the third streetcar, and walked two blocks along the sidewalk, then turned through a gate in a brick wall. A flagstone walkway wound between lawns broken by flowerbeds and shrubs, and ended at a massive stairway leading to a columned portico with arched double entry doors. Blackwell rang the bell and waited. Footsteps sounded inside.

There was a click of the latch, and the door swung open silently. A man in a suit and tie stood looking at the large and small copies of the same image. He pursed his lips to keep from smiling.

Blackwell said, "George Mason?"

The man said, "No, sir. I'm Jacobs. Robert Jacobs. May I tell Mister Mason who is calling?"

Blackwell smiled and nodded. "Please tell him Henry Blackwell is here from Portland. This is his nephew, Toby Mason."

Respect flooded the man's face. "Step this way, if you will. Mister Mason is in his study at the moment. Wait, and I will announce you."

George Mason hurried out to meet his guests. "Blackwell! Glad you got here. Walters is anxious to see you. He gave you a glowing recommendation. He will be joining us for dinner."

He called, "Jacobs! Kindly show Blackwell to his guestroom."

George Mason was a robust man with a personality to match. He turned his attention to Toby. He dropped to one knee. "Young man, I'd like to welcome you to Chicago. Just looking at you, I can see you are Jimmy's boy. Do I give you a hug, or shake your hand?"

Toby smiled. "My father always hugged me. Mother only shook my hand."

"She would." As Uncle George glanced at Blackwell, a stern look crossed his face, but gave way to a smile as he gathered the boy into a bear hug. "If it's all right with you, Toby, we demonstrate love in this house. I won't kiss you, but your Aunt Janet will. Do you mind a little kissing to go with a hug now and then?"

Toby shook his head. "Wouldn't that show that I'm wanted, instead of a bother?"

Uncle George gathered Toby into another hug, and planted a kiss on his forehead. "Changed my mind, Toby. You are no bother. We are glad to have you here."

A woman's voice tumbled down the staircase. "George, Jacobs tells me Toby has arrived. Is he here?"

Uncle George, winking at Toby, called out, "It's either Toby, or a good copy! Come on down, Honey."

Toby saw a slim woman slide down the curving banister and hop off in time to gallop down the last three stairs. With her momentum, she slid across the wood floor, scooped the boy up in a motherly hug. She whirled him around, kissed him, and set him on his feet again. "Welcome, Toby! I'm your Aunt Janet. We have some weeks before school starts, and we are going to have some adventures. Your Uncle George works too much with other people's money. I'm glad you are here so I will have somebody to play with.

"When school starts, what do you want to learn? What do you want to do?"

"I want to write stories, and maybe books. I can think them, but I want to learn to write them so people will want to read them."

Uncle George laughed. "I made a good choice, then. The school you will attend has produced some very good writers. Some write for newspapers at first, then have stories published in magazines. Those writings don't seem to take as much work or time. Sam Clemens likes to come and teach a class each year or so. They get other writers in as well. Work hard, Toby. Learn your writing craft, and you can outdo them all! You might even teach a class yourself."

Aunt Janet asked, "Did you ever teach anybody anything, Toby?"

He nodded. "I was teaching Ginny to speak correctly. I taught her to swim, too."

A mischievous smile crossed Aunt Janet's face. She whispered, "Did you wear anything?"

Toby shook his head. "Not at first. Then Missus Howard made us some swim clothes. She said I would protect Ginny's dignity if we wore them."

Aunt Janet filled the room with merry laughter. "I always wanted Uncle George to swim like that with me. That would be a real adventure. But he won't."

Uncle George said solemnly, "Janet, Dear, if you find me a pond with bushes all around it, I just might be tempted."

It was Toby's turn to laugh. "That's where we swam. There is a big pond in the willows below the house. You should go there. That's where Ginny went to take her bath for church on Sunday. I taught her to swim, and we had a race. She won."

Aunt Janet said, "I just might claim that as a promise, George. Next summer..."

"I did not promise, Janet. I said I just might."

Aunt Janet winked at Toby. "I have a witness, George. I think it is a promise. We'll go to inspect that house next summer." She reached and hugged her husband. "There. That seals it!"

Uncle George looked over Janet's shoulder to Toby. "We men are doomed, my boy. Once a girl makes us promise something, or thinks she does, we are honor bound to see she gets what she wants. Is that pond warm enough to swim in it?"

Toby nodded. "In the summer, it is. Then there are big rocks where you can sit in the sun and get dry."

Uncle George bent and kissed Aunt Janet.

Toby's brow drew into a bit of a frown. "Is a kiss a promise?"

Uncle George said, "It can be."

Aunt Janet said, "It is. Absolutely. Why? Did you kiss Ginny?"

Toby nodded. "But I didn't say I promised anything. She asked, 'Is that a promise?' and I said, 'It's a promise.'"

Uncle George shook his head. "Son, you've done it now. You signed a blank contract. Ginny gets to decide what you promised. Didn't my brother warn you about girls?"

"No. We never talked about them."

"Well, now you've been warned. Oh, I should warn you that there will be girls at your school. They are all right, but watch out, my boy. No promises!"

He kissed Aunt Janet again.

WHISTLE PIG

CHAPTER TWELVE

Pete and Ginny sat at the table after Cookie cleared the breakfast dishes. "Tell me, Ginny, what do you see out the window?"

"I kin see them there trees, but I ain't knowin' what kind they are."

Pete nodded. She eyed Ginny, with one brow raised. "Honey, I've noticed that when you are not thinking about it, when you are relaxed and comfortable, the hills come back into your speech. Then when you do think about it and correct yourself, you call attention to the hills. Will you be patient with me if I correct you, and point things out to do that?"

"I kin try."

"Can instead of Kin. I can try."

"I can try. Sorry."

"There is no need for you to be sorry,

Ginny. You said that you wish to learn to speak correctly. You learned to speak the way you do over several years, and you have had several years of practice. It will take time to change the way you speak, and I have to be the one to point out what you must change. That does not mean anything except that you must use different words.

"I think you said you want to write stories. I have an idea. I think you and I should have school right here this year. We can work on both of the things you want. You tell me stories. That way we will be able to work on your storytelling, and on your speech. I'll get you a book to help you learn more words, too."

"Just you and me? That means I wouldn't have to talk in front of other kids, and have them laugh at me. Miss Peters always laughed at the way I talked. She would imitate what I said, in a funny voice, and then everybody would laugh at me."

Pete sensed the hurt behind what Ginny shared. "Honey, that was very wrong of Miss Peters. I will not laugh at you, but I will correct you. It will not be to hurt you. It will be to save you from more hurt. If you get frustrated, I'll hug you. If you get so frustrated that you cry, I'll hold you. Will that be all right?"

Ginny nodded. "Does that mean you'll love me? Like Jesus does? Will Jesus be huggin' me if you do?"

"Bless you, Ginny, that's exactly what it

means. Jesus can sure use my arms to hug and hold you. The Bible says God disciplines every child He receives. It says that it is those He loves that He disciplines. Disciplines means he teaches and trains. That's what I will be doing for you. God is always seeking the best interest of those He loves. I will be trying to prepare you for what life holds for you when you are older.

"So, let's get started. Tell me about where you lived. Make word pictures so I can see it in my mind."

Ginny gazed out the window, thinking. Her eyelids closed halfway. Her voice was dreamy when she finally spoke. "It was as if somebody scooped out the Willamette Valley, and tossed the dirt aside in hills and wrinkles. We lived on a slope above one of those wrinkles. A spring poured out of the ground, and a little stream wandered down the valley in the sunshine to git warm. Then it crawled into the willows and curled up in a pond to nap in the afternoon sun. It was a happy stream, a-cause it woke up and went chuckling and giggling on down the valley."

Tears blurred Pete's eyes as she wondered that Miss Peters could laugh at a child's mind that could dream such a verbal tapestry. "That's beautiful, Ginny. I can see it. You are already a storyteller. Did you have any friends in the valley?"

Pete's words had not broken the spell. Ginny continued, "Below the pond was a boulder patch. Whistle pigs had dug holes under the boulders for shelter and pertection, a-cause they was feeble folks. They would sneak up out of their holes, and peek around. Then they would slide out low to the ground, and lie on their bellies to see if there was any danger. One of the older ones would climb up on a big rock, and stand up straight, looking all around. The others would creep out and start a-eatin' on the grass. If the one on the boulder saw anything dangerous, he would holler, "Chink-um! And they would all disappear into their holes. I could talk to them. We would chink-um back and forth, and they did not laugh at me."

Pete had entered into Ginny's dreamy state. She was in the valley. She was the squirrel standing guard on the boulder. As she gazed at the girl across from her, she said softly, "Chink-um!"

Ginny still sat, eyes half closed, gazing beyond the trees, beyond the city buildings, south, ever south down the valley to the wrinkle in the hills. She replied, "Chink-um!" With that, the spell was broken.

Pete's pencil had flown across her pad of paper, recording in shorthand the words of the storykeeper across from her. Later, she wrote it out in longhand, and took it to Hiram's library. "Mister Smith, I want you to read this. I asked Ginny to tell me about where she lived. This is the result."

Hiram Smith read the short description, then gazed at the governess. "Pete, she said she wants to write stories. She has a gift. The Lord has blessed her with an eye that sees as others cannot, and yet she draws them into her vision. Can you work with her? Teach her?"

Pete said, "That is what I came to discuss with you. She went to school, and the teacher and the other students mocked her. I see her as one of God's gems, but a gem that has to be carefully taken from the matrix of the hills, so the glory of Christ can shine through without the distraction of her speech. I propose to keep her here this year, so I can correct her speech and catch her up in her learning. I feel that because she was different, she was ignored. She is lacking in academic skills, but not in intelligence. May I work with her, just the two of us, for a year? Maybe more?"

"Pete, I cannot pay you enough to rub the balm of love on the scars that child carries. And she's only eight! Blackwell told me the girl's mother made her a dress of flour sacking, and that was what she wore to school. They were dirt poor. Ginny did not have any small clothes to wear under that dress. He said that one day a boy got a stick and lifted the hem of Ginny's dress so everybody saw her bare bottom. They all laughed, but that boy who was here, Toby, grabbed the stick and thrashed the boy who embarrassed Ginny. Then Miss Peters wholloped Toby, and scolded Ginny for not having under garments. There are more scars than we know, Pete. It's our duty to love the hurt out of them. Love can get to them, even if we don't know they are there."

"Well, now, you don't need to pay me to love that girl. You know what the apostle Paul wrote, don't you? **'The love of God is shed abroad in our hearts by the Holy Ghost which is given unto us.'** That 'shed abroad' means it is not a puddle inside of us. It flows through us to those He loves. We just can't help it."

Hiram nodded. "Amen to that, Pete. We'll do it. Love her, but be that squirrel on the rock, Pete. Part of loving is being on guard."

Pete smiled. "I'll have to get back up there. Do you have a word book we could borrow? A thesaurus?"

Hiram stood, running his finger along the spines of the books on his lowest shelf. "I do. I have two of them. Here, take this one. It has bigger print, and will be easier for her to read." From a higher shelf, he pulled a child's *Stories from the Bible.* "Here, take this, too. Have her read stories to you out loud. Have her read them dramatically. That will help her with fluency and with her story telling."

When Pete entered the sitting room, Gertrude stood over Ginny, her hands on her hips. Ginny turned frightened eyes on Pete, who called "Chink-um!"

Ginny ducked past Gertrude, and scurried into her room.

Auntie Gert turned to face Pete. "And what in the world was that you said?"

"I warned her in a way she would

understand that she was in danger. What are you doing in my suite? You know it is forbidden."

"I'll have you know this is my home, and you are a mere functionary. How dare you speak with such impudence? I'll tell Hiram that I expect him to fire you, and replace you with someone who knows her place."

"Mister Smith is in his library. We will go there now, and I will stand there and listen to you tell him."

"Why you… We will do no such thing."

Being of equal stature to Gertrude, but in superior condition, Pete seized her arm, and forced the irate woman out of her quarters, and headed her downstairs. As they neared the bottom of the staircase, Pete called, "This way if you would, Mister Smith. We have a problem."

Hiram came striding out of the library. "Gertrude, I have forbidden you. What is the meaning of this defiance?"

"Hiram, I want this woman fired. Get someone who knows and will keep her place. This woman was not only impudent to me, she dared to lay hands on me and force me down here."

"Gertrude, it was better her than me. I will tell you this. I employed Helen Pierce to be an escort and protector of Ginny. She has the ability to be those things. You have not yet sampled her skills. Had you resisted, she would have thrown you bodily out of the quarters. She has my permission to do just that."

"If she tried it, I would slap her silly!"

"That would be foolish on your part, but you have my permission to try it. Right here. Right now. And take the consequences."

With compressed lips, Auntie Gert drew back her hand, and swung it with all her strength. She cried out in pain as her wrist was caught in an iron grip, and she found herself spun around with her hand between her shoulder blades. Pete gave her a light push as she released her, and Auntie Gert went stumbling across the room.

Hiram continued, "I will not fire her. I have given her her tasks, and that includes guarding Ginny from you. She has learned well from those from Asia. If need be, Gertrude, she can kill you with her bare hands. I will tell you straight out. Stay away from Ginny. You wanted a marriage of companionship. We share the same roof, but you are restricted to your apartment. You wanted money, but disdained true companionship. That was your choice. Stay in your own part of the house. And stay away from the girl. This incident will go to Mister Blackwell. That is one mark against you, Gertrude. He is keeping count."

A flicker of fear crossed the woman's face. She turned, and retreated.

Pete climbed the stairs. Ginny was not in the sitting room. She did not seem to be in her own room either. Pete called, "Ginny, where are you?" Concern crept into her voice.

Ginny stirred, then crawled from under the bed. "You said to hide."

Pete scowled. "I did? All I said was chink-um."

Ginny giggled nervously. "It was the way you said it. Say it one way, and it means 'What was that?' and everybody stands up and looks around. Say it another way, and it means 'No danger.' But the way you said it means 'Hide!' and everybody runs for cover."

Pete laughed. "I did not know I spoke squirrel so well! But what you did was right. What did she want?"

"She said we are not wanted here, and she was going to take me to San Francisco where we are wanted. She said she would drag me there by the hair if she had to."

"Ginny, I'm sorry. I'll be the squirrel on the rock. I'll have to watch her as though she were a hawk, waiting to pounce on my little girl. If I say 'chink-um' you either run for Uncle Hiram, or get behind me. But stand way back, because feathers are going to fly."

∧ ∧ ∧

In Chicago, August had given way to September, and the last petals of September were falling to the floor. Toby had learned the car numbers that took him to and from school, and with Aunt Janet he had learned the streets of his neighborhood.

One afternoon, he had walked home and announced, "The wind off the lake carries knives."

Uncle George had raised an eyebrow at the figure of speech. "That is an appropriate way of stating the fact, Toby. Very descriptive. Very poetic. Use things like that in your writing. But that reminds me. I doubt you had real winters where you lived. You think the wind carries knives now, wait until January or February. Toss out a cup of hot water, and it will freeze before it hits the ground. I think the only clothes you brought are fine for summer. I'll have Aunt Janet take you shopping for things that will keep you warm when the snow flies. Then you will need some things a little lighter for spring. You can let her know what colors you like."

Aunt Janet was a fun companion, Toby decided. They shopped, then stopped at a bakery for sweet treats. She bought a large cinnamon roll for Uncle George. "This is his favorite. He would not forgive me if I got home without it. Well, for fifteen seconds, anyway."

Toby laughed. "He does not stay mad very long, does he?"

Aunt Janet became serious. "Not over little things. But there are some things he does not tolerate. He stays on them until they are set right. And he despises hypocrisy."

Toby frowned. "What's that?"

Aunt Janet sighed. "It is pretending to be something you are not. Always be true and real, Toby. Be honest in all you do, and all you say, and all you write."

"Can I write pretend stories, and still be honest?"

"Fiction, you mean. Yes, you can. You can write stories where you make everything up, or stories that are real, but you change names and things so you don't hold anybody up as objects of laughter or scorn."

"So I could write a story about when Ginny and I swam without swim clothes?"

"You could, Toby. Give yourselves other names, and write about it saying 'he' and 'she'. That is called third person writing. If you write 'I' and 'we', that is first person. People would rather have you write as someone outside the story, telling the story that way. It is fiction, but it is still honest."

Toby nodded. In his mind, he was back in the pond with Ginny. "Some day, I'd like to go back to the valley. I know Ginny won't be there, but I'd like to go anyway. I could think and remember."

"I'll talk to Uncle George. Maybe we could go next summer. Uncle George could write to Henry Blackwell, and maybe he could arrange for Ginny to visit the valley at the same time. We could stop in Portland and take her down with us. We will see what he thinks. But summer is far away. We get a long winter here, and we have to get ready for it. I'm having your clothes delivered to the house."

When they arrived home, Uncle George met them at the entry. "Toby, why don't you come in here with me?" He turned and entered the library. "I have difficult news for you, Toby. In August, I got this telegram from your mother."

Toby read, "Taking steamer *Wilma Dee* to Portland." Toby glanced at Uncle George.

He handed Toby a newspaper, folded so the headline was prominent. "*Wilma Dee* Weeks Overdue, Feared Lost."

Toby looked his question to Uncle George.

"It means they think the ship sank in the ocean, Toby. That means your mother may have died in the waves."

Toby's eyes opened wide. "But she did not love Jesus! She hated my father to talk about Him!"

Aunt Janet had followed Toby. Now, she came to kneel beside him with her arm around his shoulders. "Toby, she knew about Jesus. She may have cried out to him as the ship was sinking. We just may never know this side of glory."

"But her life was all, what did you say? Hypocrisy."

"That's between her and Jesus, Toby. You be true and honest, so that you honor her memory."

Toby nodded, then rose to go to his room. He left with a newly-budding dignity. He was solemn when he came to dinner.

Uncle George said, "Toby, I'm your legal guardian. If indeed your mother went down with that steamer, you are alone in the world. I want you to pray about something. I would like to adopt you, Toby. That way, I would step into your father's place, and Aunt Janet would step into your mother's place. You pray about it, and I will not say anything more about it until I hear from you on the subject."

Toby looked from Uncle George to Aunt Janet. He tried to see his father sitting in his uncle's chair. His uncle was bigger and jollier, but the war might have taken all the jollies out of his father. Aunt Janet was far merrier than his mother.

He could not envision his mother sliding down the banister!

He nodded. "I will. And I will say something about it. But not now."

WHISTLE PIG

CHAPTER THIRTEEN

In Portland, the passing years worked their transforming miracle in Ginny's body. She had arrived at eight as an unformed collection of twigs, a blank canvas awaiting the Creator's brush strokes of beauty. No single brush stroke gave a complete portrait. At ten, she complained to Pete, "My feet are too big." At twelve, it was "My legs are too long," and at fourteen, "My bottom is too big," and, "I'm awkward." When she was sixteen, "I'm too fat!" At eighteen, her baby fat had melted away. Her round face became an oval. At eight, she could lie down in the bath tub. At sixteen, her feet rested against one end, and her back leaned against the slope of the other end. Her clothes that had hung high in her closet now nearly reached the floor.

With the passing of those same years, the patient working of Helen Pierce shaped a blossoming intellect. The speech of the Ozarks faded into the past, giving way to a fluent and cultured communication. She had devoured the thesaurus, which was sweet in her mouth, and enriching in her mind. At eight, her handwriting had been almost infantile. At twelve, it was flowing and legible. At fourteen she had mastered shorthand, and Uncle Hiram had presented her with a typewriter. At sixteen, her nimble fingers had danced over the keys, until at eighteen she was a proficient stenographer and typist. She was also a proficient pianist, and filled the home with the classics.

At eighteen, Ginny wrote a story depicting life in the valley that had been her home. Pete read it, then said, "Ginny, this is really good. May I show it to Uncle Hiram?"

The girl had reluctantly agreed. Uncle Hiram took the pages and began an absent-minded survey, only to be drawn into the scene. Ginny's characters arose from the paper and played out their drama in his mind. He read it again. "Pete, kindly ask the girl to come down here."

When Ginny entered the library, Uncle Hiram said, "Honey, this is very well written. I want you to think about something. You said when you first came here that you wanted to write stories. I have a friend in San Francisco who is a literary agent. With your permission, I would like to share this with him. I have no doubt that through his contacts, you could have this published. A magazine would gladly buy it."

Ginny looked puzzled. "Buy it? For money? But it is just a story."

"It is a story, but it paints a word picture of an aspect of life out here, a picture that comes alive in your mind as you read it."

"But people would see my name, and some people might not like it."

Uncle Hiram nodded. "That is true, Ginny. But you could do the same thing Sam Clemens did. Use a pen name. You could hide your identity behind a name you make up. You are Virginia Garrett. How about Virgil Garrison? Use a fellow's name, and nobody would have any idea you were really Ginny Garrett. You could keep this one. You have a typewriter. You could type me another copy to send south. What do you say?"

Ginny thought, then said, "As long as I can hide behind something, you may send it. I'm just me. I do not care for any worldly fame."

Uncle Hiram smiled. "That's my girl. I admire your humility as much as I admire your accomplishments. Let me find out what Harold Nobles thinks of your writing. But, I must warn you. This is good enough that he may want more. He may want to meet you, and serve as your personal agent. If that is the case, you will have a future in literature, my girl."

Christmas was only a week away when Uncle Hiram laid a wrapped package at Ginny's place at the dinner table. When she came down the stairs, she sat and asked, "What's this?"

Hiram Smith laughed. "Open it and see!"

Ginny untied the ribbon, and pulled away

the wrapping, revealing a magazine. Emblazoned across the cover, in two inch gold letters, was "Chink-um!" Beneath the title, she read, "Page 18."

Ginny thumbed to the page indicated, and across the two-page spread she saw the title, "Chink-um!" and under that, the name Virgil Garrison.

Ginny turned to Uncle Hiram. "They wanted it? They liked it enough to print it?"

Uncle Hiram silently handed her a letter. Unfolding it, she read, *Hiram, where in the world did you find this writer? This piece is genius. It is well written. It was print ready. I had three bidders for the story, and it sold for two thousand dollars. The buyer wants to see anything else the author writes.*

The editor remarked over the way the story moves back and forth so fluently between the Ozark dialect and the general American. It is written with precision, he says, and he is amazed at the robust vocabulary, varied, but without being pretentious.

Kindly convey my desire to represent this writer in future efforts. I am enclosing an open-dated rail ticket that will facilitate a meeting here in San Francisco after Christmas and New Years are past.

I have enclosed the check from the editor, made to you in case the article came under a pen name. We can make legal arrangements when we meet early next year. Enjoy the glorious season, Hiram.

Harold Nobles

Literary Agent

Ginny's face betrayed her amazement. "They paid two thousand dollars for that story? How will they get their money back?"

Hiram Smith laughed. "Look at that cover, Ginny. Doesn't it make you want to pick up the magazine and read it? If you did not know those friends of yours, wouldn't you want to find out what in the world chink-um means? And the story itself. Once someone reads it, how many will say to someone else, 'You've just got to read this story!' They will sell plenty of magazines, Ginny. Money will pour into their account."

"But it's just a story! I made it up. Well, I lived it."

"That's just it, Ginny. It's so real. It shows a facet of life people can live without the poverty and suffering. That's why it sells.

"More than that, it embodies courage in the midst of adversity. It shows faith in action, in circumstances where faith might fail. It's not just the story. It's what lies behind the scene, behind the action. You have portrayed such sympathetic characters that people will be enticed to look for such qualities in those around them."

∧ ∧ ∧

Toby pulled the suit he had worn when he arrived in Chicago from the back of his closet. "Why have I kept this all these years?" He took the pants off of the hanger, and pushed his arm down one leg. "I got it in, but I can't bend it!" He held the pants at his waist. They did not stretch halfway across, and hung just above his knees. He shook his head. "Ginny didn't even see this on me! Wait! She did! I tried them on at the store!"

A slow smile spread across his face. "It would be quite funny to see her face if I showed up in the same outfit. I could get the tailor to make it up in my size. Pa would do it, and Ma would giggle until Christmas!" Uncle George and Aunt Janet had adopted him, and he had given them the titles Ginny had called her parents. Why, he did not know. "Odd how that girl wanders around in the canyons of my memory. I wonder if she's changed. Grown up, sure, but what about her personality?"

He sighed, and hung the ten-year-old suit back in the closet. "I'll do it. But I don't know when

I'll be going back, and if I'll find her." Toby flexed his arm. "Scrawny. But I'm still growing. I'll wait until I know I'm going. The new suit has to fit me." He tried to recall what Ginny was wearing when they left the Portland store. "Velvet, I think. Blue, like my suit." He closed his eyes, and his mind pulled out a picture of Ginny in a navy blue dress, with her round face above and black boots below. And brown curls. Then the picture faded until all that remained were pleading eyes. He heard the echo, "Will you remember?" He did. He recalled the good-bye kiss, the soft lips and the clean scent of her. He had kissed her again. He thought, "Would I? Would I dare? Would she?"

His mind left Ginny, and turned again to his story. It seemed so flat, so distant. He had stayed after class and showed it to the guest speaker, Samuel Clemens. Clemens read the piece, then had gazed out the window. Finally, he handed the pages back, saying, "Too much fog. I cannot see it."

Clemens had then said, "Son, there's no life in it, with all that death. Go there. In April. Lie on the ground. I want to know how it looks, how it feels, how it sounds, and yes, how it tastes. Be one of those wounded men. What do they fear? What do they want most? Bring out the reconciliation part. Bring it to the forefront. Bring the story to life, or bury it."

Brusque words from a man who knew writing had stirred Toby to his core. He began planning. On a shelf upstairs was a thunder mug.

How often had some pirate set off a blast of black powder in that thing? He would have it thunder across the battlefield at dawn, like the cannons of the attackers. He would smell the smoke, and imagine the scene. He would know, and then he would be able to write.

The first weekend in April, Toby left the train and boarded a steamer that would take him up the Tennessee River to Pittsburgh Landing, and followed his map to the heart of the Shiloh battlefield. He spent the day wandering from the Shiloh Meeting House to the Peach Orchard. That evening, he sat beside the Bloody Pond, imagining thirst, but recoiling from the red-tinged water. He gnawed the hard tack he had purchased. As darkness fell, he lay on the grass in the Hornet's Nest. Through the night, he resisted the canteen he had brought. The discomfort of the hard ground made him James Mason, wounded Union soldier. Near dawn, he sipped water from his canteen, and imagined the conversation with Eddie Garrett.

As the sun rose, he lit the fuse at the bottom of the thunder mug. Flame belched from the top of the mug, and the explosion rolled across the terrain. He stood to step into the cloud of smoke, and heard an agonized yell from across the field. Curious, he left what encampment he had endured, and walked toward the source of the yell. He found an old man in a gray kepi kneeling at the snake fence, weeping.

When he touched the shoulder of the grieving man, he got no response, except that the man changed from weeping to a babbled prayer. Toby waited a moment.

"Sir, I did not mean to disturb you. Do you come here often?"

The man turned his head. "I do. Every April. I see it all again. I feel it. I hear it. You are just a kid. Why are you here?"

Toby pulled out his father's letter. "This brought me here. Please read it. I was not here back then, but my father was. I came to try to understand."

The former Confederate turned and sat against the fence. "They rebuilt this fence. It was blown to pieces." He took the letter, and read it in the light of the rising sun. It dropped from nerveless fingers. He stared across toward the Bloody Pond. Drawing a shuddering breath, he said, "Eddie Garrett was my childhood friend. I saw him go down. I searched over there for his body in the night, but I could not find him. I have come here to grieve every April, and now I find he lived."

He reached for the fallen paper, and finished reading. Without looking up, he asked, "Who is Virginia?"

Toby said, "His only child. Both of her parents are dead, now. She lives in Portland with an aunt and uncle. She would be eighteen now. I have not seen her in ten years."

The old soldier talked well into the afternoon

about the events of that early April. Through his reverie, Toby relived the horror that saw thousands of men killed or missing, and countless others maimed in body and mind. Yet in the middle of that darkest of nights, enmity was melted into brotherhood. The sun was descending when the old confederate slowly folded the paper and handed it to Toby. Together they crossed to where Toby lay through the hours of darkness, and once he had gathered his gear, they headed toward the landing. Neither spoke on the long walk.

At the dock, they exchanged addresses, shook hands, and parted. Toby boarded the steamer that would take him to the Chicago-bound train, the story already morphing into a reconciliation piece in his mind. He pulled out a sheet of paper, and began trying to capture the thoughts. His neighbor's childhood friend was his ghost writer, guiding his meditations and pencil.

May was ending when Samuel Clemens spoke to the class again. Afterward, Toby walked forward and stood respectfully, waiting. Clemens looked up and asked, "Been to Shiloh, Son?"

Toby nodded, and handed his story to the old writer. Clemens adjusted his glasses and read the pages. He read them again, then grabbed a pencil and wrote a single word at the top of the title page: STET.

Toby started to ask a question, but was silenced by Clemens holding up his hand. "Don't touch it, Son. I wish I had written it myself. I'd like to buy the rights to it, and sign my own name to it. But that would make my whole life a lie. You have captured the very soul of reconciliation. There's too much hatred still swirling around the country, even after all these years. Publish this, and you will pour oil on the raging waters drowning humanity here. Here. This is the address of the office of Bub Abbott." He scrawled a note on the top of the title page. "He's an agent for writers and those who think they are. You are a real one. Tell him I said so."

It was two weeks before Toby could get in to see Abbott. When Toby was shown in, Abbott looked up and said, "Make it quick, kid. I don't have time to waste on juvenile ramblings. Why are you here?"

Toby hesitated.

"Well? Don't just stand there!"

"Sam Clemens said I should come and see you, Sir."

Abbott slapped his hand on his desk. "If there is one thing I cannot abide, it is a name dropper! How would you know a man like Samuel Clemens?"

"He is a guest instructor at my writing class."

Abbott snorted. "I'm sure he is. He takes turns with Father Christmas, no doubt. Well, what do you have there?"

Toby handed him the folder with his handwritten story.

Abbott read the note at the top: *Take this, Bub, or regret it. -- Sam*

Respect tinged the glance he gave Toby. He started to read, and halfway down the first page, he asked, "Don't you have a typewriter?"

Toby said, "I do, but I'm not very good with it yet."

Abbott bellowed, "Jane! Step in here!"

A girl a little older than Toby hurried into the office.

"Jane, type me a copy of this. I want to read it without taking time to unscramble the handwriting."

Tears streamed down the girl's face when she returned. She laid the papers on the desk, and hurried out.

Abbott read the pages without comment, then stood and reached for Toby's hand. "Son, you have done it. This is an overworked theme, but you have transcended the common trash. I'll offer you the standard contract to represent you as your agent. I'll start the bidding on this at five thousand dollars. It will sell for far more than that, and I can tell you it will resonate at the highest level in this country. Where can I reach you?"

Toby was amazed at the sudden change. "I

live with George Mason here in Chicago."

"Mason, eh? All right, my attorney will be there this evening. What name do you want to use when this is published? Because it will be."

"I'd like to use the names of the two men who were wounded. I'll be Garrett James. Eddie Garrett was the Confederate, and my father, James Mason, was the Union soldier."

Abbott pointed to a chair. "Sit there, Son. I want to know how you captured the pathos and grit of the scene."

"I was there, Sir."

Abbott stared. "You are too young to have been there."

"I went there." Toby gave an account of Samuel Clemens' first response to his efforts. "I couldn't bury it. I had to make it come alive. I met an old man who had come there to Shiloh to grieve year after year."

"Did you talk to him?"

"I showed him this letter. Then I listened." He handed his father's letter to Bub Abbott. "This letter was the seed that would not die. I had to write the story."

Abbott read the letter, then started taking notes on a pad. "We'll title it simply Shiloh. One word." He started listing names under the title. "I can think of twenty editors who will try to outbid each other for this. I cannot believe someone so young could capture the...the...Not being a soldier, how did you make it live?"

"I lived it. I lay on the ground at the Hornet's Nest, and I became Eddie Garrett. I became James Mason. I entered into the mind and heart of that old rebel who was there. In his story, I lived it, Mister Abbott."

"Do you want anyone to know that Garrett James is Toby Mason?"

"No, Sir. I'd like to remain anonymous. It's their story, not mine."

WHISTLE PIG

CHAPTER FOURTEEN

Excitement vied with uncertainty as Ginny prepared to travel to San Francisco. Helen Pierce took her to have a linen suit tailored for her meeting with Harold Nobles. The thought of meeting such a seemingly important man gave her butterflies. For that matter, the idea of a journey to another state kept them stirred up.

As the day of departure approached, Uncle Hiram called her to the library. "Honey, I'm sending Pete with you. She has done a bit of traveling herself, and knows all of the ins and outs of train travel. She has the car numbers that will take you from the train station to the hotel.

"I'm also sending Henry Blackwell with you. He knows Harold Nobles, and he will handle the legalities of the agency arrangement. He will be the one to approve any contracts before you sign them. If they want more articles, be sure you have the time you will need to write them. The faster you write them, the poorer their quality will be."

Ginny smiled. "I have two more already written. Shall I take them with me?"

Uncle Hiram thought a moment, then said, "Take one. Keep the other one in reserve. Sometimes you are a writer, and sometimes you are a thinker. When your mind is watching the characters develop the story, you watch and listen. You don't write."

Ginny giggled. "Are you a writer, too? That is exactly what is going on in my mind these days. There are two stories playing out, ripening for writing. You must be a mind reader!"

Uncle Hiram shook his head. "No, Honey, I'm no writer. I got that bit of wisdom and insight from a fellow named Sam Clemens. He stopped by Harold's office once when I was there. You may have heard of him. He writes under the pen name Mark Twain. He says he saves a lot of money other folks spend at the theater. Said he carries the theater in his hat."

Ginny shook with silent laughter. "I know the reality of that! My own imaginations entertain me. I feel sorry for those who have to have actors on a stage to act out stories."

Uncle Hiram nodded. He rose, and Ginny walked with him from the library to the foot of the staircase. They paused. Ginny had one foot on the bottom step as Uncle Hiram continued. "Watch people, Ginny. On the street corner, in the shops or on the train. Story seeds are there."

"I know. I carry a notepad and pencil. With shorthand, people around me have no idea I'm recording the scene and conversation. I have several notepads full of story seeds."

"And a fertile mind where they can germinate and grow. But, back to business, Ginny. You are going to be a surprise to Harold. He does not know you are a girl, and he does not know you are only eighteen. Present yourself with poise and confidence. He only knows you as Virgil Garrison. I told him to be ready for anything. You are nervous. I know him. He is just as nervous. My guess is that he fears you only had that one story in your head. Look at the two new ones you have. Show them to Pete, and she can help you choose the best one. Impress him with your confidence and youth."

Uncle Hiram paused, then said, "Pete will be your protection. She will not smother you, but she will always be near. Trust her instincts, Ginny. And your own. You ladies are intuitive. A man is wise who trusts the feelings and insights of a girl. Many a man has ignored them to his shame or regret."

Ginny scampered up the stairs, and found Pete packing a small trunk and a grip. She looked up and said, "I divided your things, Ginny. I put your night dress and comb and things in this grip. Oh, and some extra undergarments. Keep this with you when you get off the train. That way, if they don't get your trunk to the hotel straight away, you will have the things you need most."

Ginny's brow furrowed. "I had not thought of that."

Pete laughed. "Honey, you only need to get caught once. Then you will always remember!"

Ginny giggled. "That sounds like the voice of experience. What did you do?"

Pete winked. "I slept in the jammies I was born with!"

Ginny pretended to gasp in astonishment. "And I thought that was for swimming! But that's what I did for years in the valley when it was so hot. I still do, sometimes. It's comfortable."

Pete nodded, an inscrutable expression on her face. "It is for swimming, when you are younger."

Ginny asked, "Did you ever...?"

Pete nodded. "When I was younger. But look at you now. Would you...?"

A look of daring colored Ginny's smile. "I would! Well, it would all depend. If I ever go back to the pond, I will. Absolutely. If the willows are still there, that is."

The southbound train clattered through towns and settlements in the Willamette Valley, its whistle shrieking at the crossings. The rhythm of the rails lulled Ginny into a creative daze. Her pencil left traceries of her thoughts on the notepad. She scanned the folds of the hills trying to recall which one had been her home. Across from her, Blackwell shuffled through papers in a portfolio, occasionally making notes. Beside her, Pete dozed, snoring softly.

Ginny's pencil flew across the page. "I'm glad she's here, but I'm glad she has her own room. But I'm glad hers and mine are joined."

Another hundred miles south, the steep-faced hills gave way to another valley, with another river. Ginny realized her pencil had been still. She wrote, "The pond. Do I dare write the pond? I put my bare bottom in the school article, but the pond? We were both naked. Do I dare write that?"

The thought set the pencil in motion. Pages later, the story was roughed out. Their nakedness was only implied, and the reader's inference was confirmed by the gift of swim clothes. Toby was a lifesaving hero, and she was the champion racer. The veil of childhood innocence gave a sweetness to the account. The reader would sense the pure delight on a hot summer day.

"I may never submit this. I will have to complete it, and see what Pete has to say. I just don't know. We were not focused on bodies. I think we would be, now. I'll save it for later."

Her writing had included Toby, without him being stage front and center. She turned her pencil, and drummed the other end on the pad. "I could write the house on the hill. Or could I? That story is not finished. Some day..."

The train stopped at a water tank to refresh the boiler, and the three took the opportunity to go to the dining car. Sitting at the table, Pete asked Ginny, "Have you used your time to advantage? Did you get any notes?"

Ginny laughed. "I did more than that. Here. Read this. It is rough, but it is a start." She handed Pete her notepad, and said, "You cannot read it, Mister Blackwell. It is in shorthand."

Pete's eyes flew back and forth, working down the page. Halfway through the story, she slowly set the notepad on the table. "Oh, dear. Oh, my. Oh, Ginny. You've done it. This is really good. You have taken me back to my childhood. There were six of us. We all escaped the heat of the day exactly as you did. It was Alexander Pierce who taught me to swim, just like Toby taught you, right down to holding me until I was in motion, then letting me go. He waded beside me in case I got in trouble. Ginny, I can feel the cool of the water. I married Sandy, years later. He was...killed."

It was several minutes before Pete could pick up the notepad and finish reading. "Ginny, you tell things that take readers to where they were at one time. You allow them to relive those things they dared. Some readers who never dared can live the experiences with you. Maybe you will give them courage to...to dare. That is what sells your stories. You lived them, and dare others to live."

Blackwell raised both eyebrows and shook his head. "And what has she been writing now, Pete?

"Skinny dipping, Henry. She wrote about skinny dipping in a mixed group."

Blackwell smiled and nodded. "Ah, yes. I remember..." His supper sat untouched as he was lost in reverie.

Pete said, "Henry! Eat!"

Blackwell jumped. "Oh, right." He cleaned his plate.

Supper was finished the next evening, and Blackwell and Ginny sat in the hotel dining room, chatting. A tall gentleman in a bowler came in from the sidewalk, and stood searching the diners for a familiar face.

Blackwell said, "Here we go, Ginny. I'll be here in a moment. That man is Nobles."

The man indicated started hesitantly across the room, zigzagging between tables. Blackwell moved to intercept him, and caught his arm.

Turning, Nobles said, "Blackwell! What are you doing here? I mean, it is good to see a familiar face."

"I'm probably here for the same reason you are, Harold."

"I'm here to meet a potential client. A writer named Virgil Garrison."

Blackwell pulled on the elbow he had seized. "Come sit with me, Harold."

As they approached, Ginny looked up and smiled. Blackwell said, "Harold, this is my ward, Virginia Garrett. She is a private person who prefers anonymity, who writes under the pen name of Virgil Garrison."

Harold Nobles stared at the teenage girl. "Is this some kind of hoax, Henry?"

Ginny kept a blank face, and said, "I ain't bin a-tryin' to mock you none, ner nothin', Mister. I jest bin a-waitin' and a-waitin fer some feller what was a-wantin ter talk to me." She rose at the look of consternation that covered Harold Nobles' face. "I'm so sorry, Mister Nobles. The temptation was just too inviting to resist. You mentioned to Uncle Hiram how you were amazed that I could slip fluently from the Ozarks to the general American dialect. I just had to authenticate my credentials, so to speak."

Harold Nobles roared with hearty laughter as he took the fingertips offered him. Other diners turned to see the cause of the commotion, then resumed their dinners and conversations. The three sat, and Nobles said, "A girl! I did not expect someone so young." Incredulity tinged his voice and face.

Ginny pulled out a portfolio. "Here is my copy of the article you had published. And here," she took another packet of papers, "is another submission that may confirm my identity, if you would like to read it."

Nobles pulled glasses from his jacket pocket, adjusted them, and read the first page. "I know you from your style, Virginia."

She interrupted him with "Please call me Ginny. It's friendlier."

Nobles started over. "I know you from your style, Ginny. You write with a precision that does not lack...what? Emotion? Heart? Sympathy? All of these and more. I am amazed. How old are you, Ginny?"

"I'll be eighteen in two months."

Nobles shook his head. "Too young."

Blackwell had not said anything, but now spoke up. "That's why I am here, Harold. I'm her guardian, by the court's decree. But Hiram wants me to serve as her attorney in any contract negotiations. But let's find a quieter place to discuss this." The two men rose. Nobles asked, "May I take this portfolio with me, Ginny?"

She nodded, and when the two went out, she sat with her pencil flying over the page in her notepad.

"May I join you, Miss?"

Ginny looked up to see a balding man in a tailored suit standing over her. "I suppose. Do I know you?"

"No, Miss. But I know of you." He took a seat in the chair Blackwell had recently occupied. "I am Archibald Parker of this city. You look like a companionable sort. I could offer you many possibilities. We could take the train to New York, and a ship to Europe. We could honeymoon in Paris, or London."

Behind her, Ginny heard, "Chink-um!"

Ginny asked, "And how do you know anything about me?"

The man squirmed a little, and said, "Your Aunt Gertrude sent me a telegram that said you would be here. She said to look for a girl with wavy brown hair, and offer her the world."

"Chink-um!"

Ginny stood. "Sir, I have never heard of those places you mentioned. However, I have heard of Death Valley. If that was a proposal of marriage, it was as devoid of God-honoring feelings needed for marriage as Death Valley is devoid of refreshing pools. You may go to Death Valley, as far as I am concerned. Pete, why don't you and I seek those two who are true gentlemen who have hearts and brains."

Helen Pierce rose from the table behind Ginny, and the two left Archibald Parker with his mouth working like a goldfish.

On the way out, Ginny said, "First, you called 'Danger!' and then you said 'Hide!' That's where we are going. I have no idea how Auntie Gert knew I would be here, or why she thought I would fall for such a clumsy line. Using the word 'honeymoon' does not include a wedding, does it?"

When they joined the two men, Nobles asked, "What did Archibald Parker want? I saw him approach your table."

Ginny snorted. "He wanted to take me to Paris or London for a honeymoon."

Nobles winced. "Ginny, they would have found your dead body in the morning."

Pete said, "Or his."

Blackwell asked, "How did he know you were here?

"He said he had a telegram from Auntie Gert."

"Gertrude. Ginny, I want you to write up an account of the meeting and conversation. I think Gertrude planned that you would disappear. Pete, you heard?"

"I did. I am a witness. Ginny caught my warning."

Blackwell nodded. "Kindly write your own account. I want independent statements. And Pete, I want you to stay close to Ginny while she is here."

Blackwell looked to Harold Nobles. "Your turn, Harold."

Nobles pulled out a chair for Ginny. On the table in the hidden corner of the entry, Nobles had an agency contract, and an agreement to supply six additional articles. The articles would be put out to bid by competing magazines. He fluttered the new submission in the air. "I have a standing starting bid of two thousand dollars. It can only go up from there. If you sign the contract, I want the article you used as your credentials. I can guarantee you two thousand, and it may reach five thousand, Ginny. Your writing is that authentic, and that good."

Ginny looked to Blackwell, who nodded slightly.

She signed.

^ ^ ^

Dinner was finished when Abbott's attorney, Joseph Watkins, was ushered into the parlor where George Mason waited with Toby. The two rose, and took the offered hand as Watkins introduced himself, saying, "Thank you for receiving me at this late hour. I'll be brief."

He took the offered seat, and pulled a sheaf of papers from his briefcase. "Mister Abbott sent a standard contract for representation. He wanted me to tell you, Toby, the bid stands at ten thousand dollars, and that is only from the houses here in Chicago. Two bids came with substantial offers for rights if you will expand the story into a book. One offer is for fifty thousand."

The look on Toby's face showed his amazement. "It's only a story! Why would anyone offer so much?"

Watkins shook his head. "I can't tell you that. Some stories fall flat. Others, well..."

Toby said, "I think I will leave it as it is, at least for now. I don't think a book would have the same impact. This is short. I don't have time to stretch it into a book. I spent a night lying on the ground in the dark at the battlefield to get this. How long would it take to soak up a longer work? Not now, Mister Watkins."

The attorney sighed, and placed one bundle of papers back in the briefcase. "Well, I tried. Here is your autograph, and a couple of typed copies. Abbott said you should keep the handwritten one as a memento, with the note from Clemens on it." He reached for the contract. "This does not demand a book from you, and it is open to future submissions without specifying a minimum number or any time frame. Abbott just wants to be the one who gets them. He would like at least four."

George Mason took the contract, read through it, and handed it to Toby. "No problem with this, Toby. I think you could sign it with ease of mind."

Toby signed.

When Watkins left, Toby shook his head. "Pa, what makes people pay such sums for so small an effort?"

"Toby, you poured yourself into that project. May I read that?"

Toby handed him a typed copy, and waited while he read it.

"Toby, this is more than a retelling of a battlefield incident. It goes straight to the heart."

"The girl who typed it was crying when she brought the copies."

"That is because the message here goes straight to inner battlefields, to hidden hurts. I'm going to guess it spoke to something in her life that needs reconciliation. That's a Bible concept. Reconciliation often takes place in the most difficult circumstances. Look at your father's case. In the darkness, enmity changed to brotherhood. Those two were surrounded by death and hurt, the dead and dying. It was thus with Christ on our behalf. The Bible says, **'For if, when we were enemies, we were reconciled to God by the death of his Son, much more, being reconciled, we shall be saved by his life.'** The believer was moved from being an enemy of God to being a child of God. God did not change to allow a sinner into His family. He drew that one to Himself, and placed the believer in His Son. As a child of God, we have a message to share. **'And all things are of God, who hath reconciled us to himself by Jesus Christ, and hath given to us the ministry of reconciliation; To wit, that God was in Christ, reconciling the world unto himself, not imputing their trespasses unto them; and hath committed unto us the word of reconciliation.'** Your article has the power to penetrate walls of division, to heal wounds no bullet can give, and to bring conviction. That is the hidden power God has used you to include in this.

"You were right to refuse the book. First of all, you don't have time and energy to make this bigger. It would take away from your schooling, or your schooling would diminish the writing. Let this have its impact. It is short. People will read it, and it will make them think. It is in the thinking that its work will be accomplished.

"People will spend money on it. The financial panic over the Philadelphia and Reading collapse is behind us, and folks are starting to part with a bit more of their cash. I lost heavily in that crisis, but not so much in the railroad directly. It was the banks that panicked, and caused other businesses to fail. The book might do the same to your article. It might take away from the pointed message."

Toby thought, then asked, "Was it honoring to use both names as a pen name? That's what I wanted."

"I'm glad you used my brother's name. I think Ginny would approve of you honoring her father as well."

"If she ever finds out. I'm not going to tell her. At least, not now."

"Write the short articles. Something called rural Americana is popular right now. There is a hunger for nostalgia. Write about your early years. Magazines are printing that now, and it takes people back to their roots. Connect with people where they were when they were younger. Touch their hearts."

Toby chuckled. "I have a couple of articles of that kind all ready, except I keep going back and changing things. I'll see what Abbott thinks."

WHISTLE PIG

CHAPTER FIFTEEN

Henry Blackwell reached and caught Ginny's wrist as she turned to head for the stairs. "Wait, Ginny. Pete, I saw Archibald Parker slip upstairs a few minutes ago. He turned twice and looked at Ginny. I want you to go up the second flight part way, and see if you can find a place to watch over the girl as she goes up."

When Pete was out of sight, Blackwell said, "All right, Ginny, up you go."

On the landing above, unseen by Blackwell and Nobles below, Ginny's scream was caught in an acrid-smelling cloth that covered her nose and mouth. Her struggles grew feeble, and she slumped to the floor. Parker was reaching for her arm as Pete clattered down the stairs from above. "Don't you touch her!"

Parker attempted to seize the onrushing woman, but he was sent pinwheeling over the landing rail. Pete's yell was drowned out by Parker's bellow of fear. The sound from below resembled that of a watermelon hitting the marble floor. Parker lay prone at the feet of Henry

Blackwell, who called to the clerk, "Better send for a doctor. And a policeman, if you can."

The clerk called, "There's a cop on beat down the block. I'll get him. We have a doctor staying on the second floor. Tell you what, I'll send the doorman for the cop. I'll get the doctor." He took the stairs three at a time. Pete knelt beside the unresponsive Ginny. She had straightened the girl's dress, and was gently slapping her cheek, trying to wake her up.

The doctor came down in pajamas and slippers carrying his black bag. He knelt beside Parker. "Fractured skull...displaced cervical vertebrae...broken arm...no pulse. Anything else?"

Blackwell said, "Kindly check the girl on the landing."

The doctor jumped. "Guess I was in too much of a hurry. I did not see a girl." With that, he was halfway up the first flight."

Ginny's breathing was slow and spaced out. Seeing the rag by her nose, the doctor grabbed it and sniffed. "Chloroform!" He motioned Pete, who had been looking on helplessly. "Help me, if you please. We have to turn her onto her side. She'll be all right, but she is going to lose her supper. We can't have her inhale any."

The doctor held the limp girl and said to Pete, "Kneel down here and brace her back." He dug down in his bag and pulled out a square of oilcloth. He grabbed a handful of Ginny's hair and lifted her head, slipping the oilcloth under her face.

By this time, Harold Nobles had reached the landing. Ginny's body drew up into a fetal position. Her breathing changed to quick gasps.

The doctor said, "Keep her braced. Here it comes."

The unconscious girl retched repeatedly, until there was nothing left to throw up. The doctor pulled a cloth from his bag and wiped her face. To Nobles he said "Pillow off that couch, please." He pulled the oilcloth aside, placed the pillow under Ginny's head, and let go of her hair.

Pete, still bracing Ginny on her side, had leaned across and planted her hand where it pinned the girl's arms. With a cry like a wounded animal, Ginny began to struggle.

Pete held her tightly and said, "Chink-um!"

Ginny drew up into a tight ball and lay still. Her eyes fluttered open, and she began to look wildly about.

Seeing Pete, the girl began to cry. "Help me!"

The doctor lifted her into a sitting position, and Pete embraced her as sobs shook Ginny's entire frame. "You are safe now, Honey. We've got you."

Blackwell, the officer and the clerk were coming upstairs. The body of Parsons was covered with a blanket, awaiting removal. The doctor said, "Does the girl have a room here?"

The clerk said, "She does. These two ladies have two sixteen and two seventeen."

"Well, get her in her bed."

Pete lifted Ginny easily, and carried her down the hall. "Two sixteen. Open the door, please." She laid the reviving girl on the bed.

The doctor rummaged in his bag, and pulled out two bottles. "Give her two of these with a glass of water tonight. She will have a terrific headache in the morning. Chloroform does that. Give her two of these other pills when she wakes up. She won't want any breakfast, but she will be quite hungry in the afternoon. I'd say she'll be clear to travel day after tomorrow."

Blackwell pulled out his wallet, and took out two bills. "This is for your house call, Doctor. I thank you."

The officer said, "You don't get any rest yet, Doc. I need you to tell me what you know." The two stepped out into the hall, and met the clerk, who handed the doctor the now-clean oil cloth.

"You cleaned up that mess? I thank you!"

In Ginny's room, Blackwell said, "Pete, get the girl tucked in. I'll stand by outside her door. The officer will want your statement. He asked me, 'How did this guy get down here?' I said, 'He flew.'

He asked me, 'Do you know who this guy is?' and I said, 'Archibald Parker.' He said, 'Nope. He's Andrew Parsons. He gets paid to kill people. We've been looking for him for three weeks now.'"

Blackwell pulled a telegram out of his shirt pocket. "Pete, I'll need you to copy this in front of witnesses. It was found in the pocket of the man who attacked Ginny. It's a message from Gertrude Smith to the man she paid to kill Ginny." He turned toward the door. "I'll wait outside. You get her undressed and tucked in." He closed the door behind him.

The officer was just dismissing the doctor. "You are next, Blackwell. You heard a struggle, and then a yell. What happened next?"

"The guy came flying over the rail and landed on his head at our feet. We hollered for the clerk to send for a doctor, and send for you. Ginny had said the man approached her and proposed a honeymoon in Paris or London. Nobles must have known something of local news. He said her dead body would have been found in the morning. We saw Parker or Parsons sneak up the stairs. His actions aroused suspicion, so I sent Pete, that's what we call Helen Pierce, up the stairs first. Hiram Smith up in Portland had said she had skills that made her valuable for protecting Ginny. I guess I did not realize those skills were lethal."

The officer chuckled. "She does not look that strong or big, but those are the ones you have to look out for! Parsons was not that puny himself.

Leverage and adrenaline, I'd say. We could use her on the force!"

Ginny's headache and nausea kept her from heading north for three days. Henry Blackwell left for Portland two days before Ginny was able to travel. He had drawn a deep breath, exhaling slowly as he looked at the girl. "Ginny, your dear Auntie will not be there when you arrive. I have gathered strong evidence of attempted murder for hire that will lock her away. I know she is family, but she may not fail next time. Pete will take care of your needs in the meantime. If your loving aunt happened to be there when Pete arrived, I would not bet on her chances of seeing the sun rise again. I'm on my way. You rest and recover. I'll see you when you get home."

Uncle Hiram held Ginny in an extended embrace when she got home. "Honey, you don't know how relieved I am to have you home again. I had no idea your aunt had connections like that in San Francisco. My stomach still gets all knotted up when I think of how close you came to being killed.

"Blackwell has it arranged so you will not have to testify, or even attend the trial. He said you were out cold, and would have nothing to contribute. The sworn statements of the other witnesses form an air-tight case. I'm sorry, Ginny. I can't say I'm sorry for her, or sorry that she will spend years in prison. I'm so sorry you had to go through what you endured."

Ginny murmured, "I'm fine." After a

moment, she said, "No, I'm not. I can't forgive her, but I have to. Pray for me, Uncle Hiram. I can't love her, but I don't want to hate her. Is there something halfway between?"

Hiram found he still embraced the girl. "Come sit beside me, Ginny."

When they were seated on the couch, Uncle Hiram crossed his ankles in front of him. Ginny hugged her knees. Hiram sighed. "Ginny, I know how you feel. When you forgive, it does not always mean that you take up life as it was before the offense. You can't get her out of prison, and you do not want to go to prison with her. Forgiving means you do not feel the need to get even, to pay her back. You turn that over to God. Your feelings toward her may never turn to the positive side, but you can come to neutral. Pity her in her lostness. You will know you have forgiven her when you find you can pray for her salvation. The scars of the incident may have to do a bit of healing before you get there. But, Honey, I will pray that becomes your reality. Please pray for the same thing for me."

Ginny leaned against his shoulder. "Thank you. That gives me a direction. My emotions and thoughts have been circling around my hurt. It was killing all of my stories, and my memories that formed them."

Uncle Hiram snapped his fingers. "Your stories! I forgot. You have news, Ginny!"

When he returned from his library, he handed Ginny two envelopes. She tore open the first, and pulled out a telegram: *Ginny, the article about the church in the valley sold for three thousand. Stop. Five bidders. Stop. Publish in three months. Stop. Nobles*

The second bore a Chicago post mark. It was from Toby. Her hands trembled as she opened it.

Hello, Ginny! I'm writing to ask you to forgive me. Uncle George and Aunt Janet decided to make a trip to our valley. Ginny blushed as she read, *Remember when I taught you to swim? Aunt Janet wanted to go to the pond to swim like we did. I heard them yelling and laughing for over an hour! Maybe...never mind. We are both bigger now.*

We were going to go through Portland and take you with us, but Uncle George had business in San Francisco, so we came up from the south instead. That was when we were ten, Ginny. I think you and I are both eighteen now. And I am only now writing.

I had only been here in Chicago a couple of months, no, less than that, when the newspaper had a headline that the steamer my mother took going to Portland was missing at sea. There has been no word of the vessel in all these years, but it has taken me that long to be able to forgive my mother for so many things. The Lord has changed my heart toward her, Ginny.

Are you writing anything? I'm studying journalism, and am writing a column for a newspaper here. I have stories trying to get out of my head. Someday, I may get them on paper. It is just that my mind goes so much faster than my pencil, and my clumsy fingers stumble over the keys on my typewriter. Someday, I may find somebody who can take dictation, and then I won't run into that pool of quicksand that swallows my stories a-borning.

I'm working on one, though. One that you ordered. It comes from my father's letter to your father. It may never be anything, but I'm trying.

I'll try to find you the next time I get to the West Coast, Ginny. Until then, Toby.

Ginny sat lost in a daydream. Toby had come. He said he would come again. She pondered the days in the pond. "Could I? Would I dare?" She tried to picture her mature self in the pond, with nothing between her and the water. In her dream, Toby was an undetailed shape beside her. They frolicked and laughed, then vanished from her mind. "No. I could not do that. I...Toby has not said anything about marrying me. That was all in my mind. That is a temptation that I must push away."

A new dream opened in her theater. She sat beside Toby. He leaned back, his fingers clasped behind his head, telling her a story. She had her pad and pencil, and caught every word, no matter how fast he spoke. They were most proper, Toby sitting at his desk, while she sat on the chair nearby. "I could do that, and then I could type his manuscript. I could!"

^ ^ ^

The Chicago church Toby attended with Pa and Ma Mason was out of step with the majority of that city's religious effort. Paul Mitchell referred to himself as pastor rather than reverend. He emphasized the grace of God rather than the works of man. He taught trust in spite of circumstances. He taught the Word of God systematically, verse by verse, thus opening the understanding of his hearers. He and the other elders worked to prepare the saints for the work of ministry.

Toby sat under the teaching of the word, and took the special classes that would prepare him to plan and deliver sermons in the same fashion. "Verse by verse. Line upon line. Precept upon precept. That's how to teach the Word. Read the Bible all the way through. Start in Genesis, and when you finish The Revelation, start over and read it again. When you speak, read the Word. Explain the Word. Apply the Word. And every day of the week, live the Word." Paul Mitchell gave the pattern Preacher John had used.

One evening, Mitchell asked Toby to stay after the others had departed. "Toby, why have you not taken classes at one of the seminaries in Chicago?"

Toby had given a simple answer. "Because of the preachers they turn out. They don't teach the truth. We are not saved by doing. We are not kept by doing. We are not made like Christ by doing. Paul told Timothy to preach the Word. They don't. They present another Jesus, another gospel. If we can save ourselves, why did Jesus die?"

Paul sat gazing at Toby. Then, he nodded silently. Finally he said, "The elders would like you to prepare a message for next Sunday morning. I'll take care of the opening. You will have forty minutes. You choose the passage, and the only instruction I will give you is to speak to the person clear in the back. That way, you will know the people closer to the front will hear you. Do you have a good library of books about the Bible?"

Toby laughed. "I do. For every book in the Bible, I have sixty-five other books that will shine light on it."

Paul Mitchell stood, and when Toby rose to go, he slapped the younger man on the back. "Perfect answer, Toby. Let the Word of God explain the Word of God. You will do fine. What is the first thing you plan to do?"

"Pray. Then pray some more. I am in no

way adequate for the task you have assigned."

The result of that message reached far into the future for Toby. The following week, he endured several hours of grilling on his beliefs, and his understanding of the Word of God. His was no memorized catechism. His was a simple statement of the truths he found within the covers of his well-worn Bible. Every answer came with Toby turning to a supporting passage and reading it. The elders surrounded him, laid hands on him, prayed over him, and ordained him to share the truth of the Word.

Paul Mitchell shook his hand, and said, "Pastor Toby, don't ever say you are Reverend Toby. That's for Jesus alone. Be humble. Be simple in your presentation. Make certain the little ones can understand."

Toby grinned. "There was a little church in the valley where I lived my early years out in Oregon. The man there was simple, humble and, well, holy. Everybody called him Preacher John. That's the only name I ever knew. He taught the older ones, but he sure loved the little ones. He has been my model. He could carry his whole library in one hand, but his preaching was living and powerful. I just pray that I will be able to measure up."

Paul Mitchell thought a moment, his forehead puckered between his eyebrows. Then his face cleared. "I read about him in a magazine article, last year, I think it was. He had a crown of white hair, a white beard, and twinkling eyes. Knew and loved Jesus."

Toby gaped. "You read about Preacher John? Who betrayed him? He was always self-effacing."

Mitchell shook his head. "I don't recall. Some fellow out in Oregon, I suppose. The writer seemed to know him. Why, Preacher John seemed to get up off those pages and walk around the room, chuckling over the antics of a couple of kids in his church."

"I can't think of anyone who would have known him that well. Unless it was someone who moved into the valley after I left. What magazine was it?"

Pastor Paul shook his head. "I don't recall. I think it was in some waiting room, maybe at one of the hospitals. They seemed to like to publish what is termed Americana."

"And somebody wrote about that little church. I doubt Preacher John is still living. I doubt any pastor has stepped up to call the folks in that valley to worship. One of these days, I'd like to open that door, sweep out the dust, and ring the old bell. Pastor Paul, some day I will do just that. I wonder who might show up. Folks used to walk or arrive in buggies."

WHISTLE PIG

CHAPTER SIXTEEN

Ginny hesitated, then dropped the letter into the box. "All these years, and we have not written. Toby's letter was short. I wonder if he will take the time to read all of the pages I wrote?" She pondered what the letter revealed. *I've written some stories, and managed to get some published. Nobody knows who I am, because I hide behind a pen name. I guess what I write would be classified Americana. I write about what I know.* That would not give away any of her accomplishment details. *Since you know the valley, you would see yourself in my stories, even though I changed your name.* He probably did not even read the magazines that had featured her stories.

Blackwell stopped to have Uncle Hiram sign three documents that evening. Ginny caught him as he was leaving. "When are you going to see Millie again?"

The attorney smiled. "I'm heading down there next week. Want to go along?"

Ginny nodded. "I have not been back in all of these years. When we went to San Francisco, I could not even remember which wrinkle in the hills I lived in. I'd love to ride along, just to find my way again."

"I leave on the Tuesday morning train. I'll buy you a ticket. We go as far as Salem, and then I'll rent a buggy. We'll drive out. I'm sure Millie will be happy to give you a room for as long as you want to stay. Jackson can drive you back to catch the train north to Portland. Or, maybe you can return with me. Pack a bag, and I'll come for you Tuesday. We board at nine o'clock." He gave Ginny a quick hug, and was gone.

Light rain fell Tuesday morning, and persisted all the way through the Willamette Valley. As the buggy crept eastward toward Aumsville, the clouds broke up, and the mist dried away. Millie heard the crunch of gravel as they stopped in the circle of the driveway. She opened the door, and stood staring. "And who have you brought with you, Mister Blackwell? No, wait. I know those eyes. Ginny! My, how you've grown up! Come on up here, and let me give you a hug!" Her motherly embrace removed Ginny's doubts about dropping in unannounced.

"Millie, you have not changed a bit!"

"Well, Honey, I certainly cannot say the same for you! You are as tall as I am, and you have left the hills behind you!"

Ginny laughed and said, "Well, I ain't bin here in a bunch o' years, but I shore bin wantin' to.

I bin a-growin' some sinst I goed away."

It was Millie's turn to laugh. "That's my Ginny, all right! Come on in, both of you. Bread's in the oven, and I'll have sandwiches in no time at all."

That afternoon, Ginny changed to a split riding skirt and blouse, and told Millie, "I'm going across to the graves, and then I'll stop by the pond."

"You do that, Honey. I get over there from time to time, and keep the weeds cleared away. I'll see you for supper."

As Ginny went down the hill, she surveyed the valley. The church still stood, but it appeared that the roof was caving in on the school building. On a whim, Ginny turned toward the willows. She had to duck low to push her way through the branches. "How in the world did Toby get through here?" Before she emerged from the tangle, she had to take off her boots and wade the last few feet. It was a short step up onto the boulder that years ago had made her scramble up on hands and knees. She stood looking down to the other end of the pond. "It looks so small, now. It took forever to swim down there when we were little."

As she gazed at the water, Ginny's hands strayed to the buttons of her blouse. "I will!"

Her clothes folded neatly behind her, she stepped into the water. Beside the boulder, the pond reached only just above her knees. "It's shallow! used to come up above my waist!" She took two steps forward. "I think it's deep enough, though."

She leaped forward, and with practiced strokes slid through the water. At the far end, she turned onto her back, and swam slowly back. She thought, "Toby! I can still do it! I wish you were here!" Then she thought, "No, I don't! Well, I do, but we have to be married first. Kin I love you, Toby? You said I could, iffen I was a-wantin' to. Well, I am, Toby. Wherever you are, and whatever you have become, I love you!" Louder, she called, "I love you, Toby Mason!"

Ginny sat on the boulder with her pile of clothes, the last of the pond water trickling from her hair and running down her back. The sun was warm on her skin, and the swirling breeze mopped up the residue of her swim. Her wavy hair gradually drew up into tighter curls. When she could toss her head without throwing water, she stood and dressed, then waded back through the willows, carrying her boots.

She circled above the willows, and hopped across the streamlet that nourished the pond, then climbed barefooted toward her old home. Grass had closed over the path. The necessary had crumpled into a jumble of boards. The roof had fallen in over the dugout earth home. She stopped, and tears blurred her vision. She stood leaning against the old oak, remembering.

Ginny climbed slowly up to the gathering on the hillside. There were more stones. Beside her father's grave, she read the stones of Preacher

John and Louise Howard. Other stones bore names she could not recall. "You were here first, Pa. Then Ma joined you. I remember Preacher John and Louise Howard tucking you in, Ma. And Toby kissed me."

Ginny closed her eyes, as she had done then. "Toby kissed me." Smiling, she sighed. "And Toby kissed me."

She walked slowly back down the slope. The grass by the streamlet was cool under her feet. "And Toby kissed me." She stepped into the cold water, delighting in the touch. "And Toby kissed me."

Ginny stepped from the stream. "Toby does not even know you! He would not recognize you! Be realistic." Her self-rebuke turned her toward the house on the hill. Over supper, she asked casually, "Millie, has Toby ever come back to the valley?"

"He did, Ginny, but it was years ago. I think he was ten. I have not seen him since. But someday, I'm certain he will come back. You did. At last." The final words were spoken softly.

"I know, Millie. I went by here once on the train, but I could not remember which wrinkle I had lived in. I came with Mister Blackwell because he knew the way." She paused, then asked, "Do you have any idea when Toby might come again? He would not know me, and I doubt I would know him. But I would not mind if our paths crossed someday. Somewhere."

Millie smiled. "He kissed you, didn't he? I seem to recall he kissed you, there in the church." She winked at Ginny. "I would not mind seeing him kiss you in the church again. But since Preacher John died, there has been nobody to ring the bell. We keep the building in good repair, waiting. Oh, and I meant to tell you. Jackson took a hammer and chisel over and chipped the letters deeper on your parents' stones."

Ginny smiled her thanks. "I thought they looked easier to read. Ma had just scratched Pa's name on his, and I heard Preacher John used a hammer and a nail for Ma's. Give Jackson a kiss for me."

Millie giggled. "You have my permission to kiss him yourself, Ginny. I've been kissing him since he asked me to marry him!"

Ginny looked at Millie. "Seriously, Millie, do you ever get tired of kissing your husband?"

"Not for very long, Honey. Not for very long! Just long enough to catch my breath!"

On the journey back to Portland, Ginny asked Blackwell, "Do you ever hear anything about Toby? Is he all right? He wrote that he was trying to write, but his stories were flat and lifeless. Will he ever be coming back out this way?"

Blackwell smiled. "George tells me he's doing well. George and Janet adopted him after his mother's ship was lost at sea. George said Toby has had some writing advice from a writer named

Sam Clemens. I think you will hear something of that young scamp before long. He's as old as you are, isn't he, Ginny? Twenty-one?"

"He is. I know that's a little young to make any kind of mark in the world, but it would be nice to cross paths with him again. He was the only one who cared anything about me in school. But that was years ago."

"Ginny, I'll ask George to keep me informed. But you never know about young kids like that. They might get a bee in their bonnet, and who knows where they might show up, or what they might do?"

∧ ∧ ∧

In his mind, Toby put the Shiloh article on the shelf. Three years had all but evaporated since he took it to Bub Abbott. Abbott had predicted a publication date sometime in May. The issues of magazines were planned for printing that far in advance. Already the calendar had turned to a new century. The war of secession had been over for almost four decades. In Toby's mind, it was old news. His thoughts turned westward.

The values of the world were on full display

in Chicago. Even in his church, the girls his age sported the latest styles, and engaged in the latest fads of speech and behavior. They were out for a good time, putting on a façade of piety on the Lord's Day, and blending into the godless frenzy about them the rest of the week. Ever between himself and the girls, he saw Ginny. He tried to imagine her as she would be at twenty-one. Would she blend in, or would she stand out?

"Someday, Ginny, our paths will cross. Will I know you?" Toby was lost in the valley in Oregon. "I kissed her." He smiled, and closed his eyes. "I kissed her. I'll do it again, Ginny girl. Some day, I'll kiss you again. It's a promise. I love you, Ginny Garrett!" There. He said it. He would tell her. Some day, he would tell her.

Bub Abbott had told Toby his article would resonate to the highest level. In the nation's capital, the president sat tapping his thick finger on the cover of a magazine. The feature article had its title emblazoned in block letters: SHILOH.

An intern stood by, waiting. "Two things. See if Pinkerton can spare a man for a research project. And I want to see Adams from engraving."

The intern vanished, but was replaced by another, in case there might be more requests. The president turned to the article again. Adjusting his thick glasses, he reread the columns, turning the pages, pausing often to picture the scenes described, and to endure the emotions they stirred.

He was interrupted in his meditation by the arrival of the Pinkerton man. "You have a project for us, Mister President?"

Theodore Roosevelt thumped the magazine. "There is an article here by someone named Garrett James. I want to know who and where he is."

"Yes, Sir. May I take the magazine?"

"No. I need it for a meeting. Get your own copy. Government expense."

"Yes, Sir. We will get that information right away."

Roosevelt read the article twice more before Adams appeared.

"You wanted to see me, Mister President?"

"I did. I do. I have a project for you. Take notes." He pushed a pad and pencil across the desk. They slid over the edge, and Adams caught them.

"I want you to design a medal. Round, two inches across. On the front, around the rim, I want it to say *United States Presidential Medal of Merit.* Then I want the stars and stripes with its staff crossing over the staff of the stars and bars. Across the flag staffs, I want the word Shiloh. All capital letters."

Adams interrupted. "Mister President, I can't do that. It would be blasphemy. My grandfather was killed at Shiloh."

TR gazed at the young man. "Still bitter about that, are you? Tell me. Did you know your grandfather?"

"No, Sir. He was killed before I was born."

"So you got your bitterness from your father?

"I guess so."

"You carry hand-me-down hatred? Is there someone in particular you hate, or do you just hate? Half of the country does that." The president picked up the magazine and opened it to the feature article. "Son, I want you to go and read this, and then bring me your sketch. Read the article first. It is the best article that features reconciliation that I have ever seen. Just what this country needs. The war is over."

Adams took the magazine, and with compressed lips, he turned and stalked out. Roosevelt told the intern, "Go to a newsstand, and bring me three more copies of that magazine." He pulled a bill out of his shirt pocket. "Take this, and keep whatever is left over for your trouble."

Three hours later, the president was napping at his desk, his head resting on the magazines, when he was awakened by the arrival of the Pinkerton man. "I have your report, Mister President."

Roosevelt yawned and stretched. "Which do I say? It took you long enough? That was fast work? What do you have for me?

"Your man is Tobias Mason of Chicago. Bub Abbott is his agent. Toby writes under the pen name of Garrett James. That pseudonym combines the names of the two soldiers in that article. Edward Garrett was the rebel. James Mason was the Union soldier, and was Toby's father. Toby's just twenty-one."

The president nodded his thanks, casually dismissing the agent. He drummed his fingers on the magazine cover. "Shiloh was a battle nobody won. Wars are like that. Nobody wins, and then everybody suffers as they pick up the pieces." He opened the magazine, and read the article again. "Just a kid. How could he know?"

Adams stood at the door. Roosevelt looked up. "Come in, Adams. Are you free yet?"

The young man crossed to the desk, and laid his sketch in front of the president. "Mister President, I thank you. That hit me plumb center. Here's your magazine."

Roosevelt shook his head. "You keep that as your banner of freedom. Now, let's look at this." He took off his glasses, wiped them and rested them on his nose. He reached for a pencil, which he handed to Adams. "Slight correction here." He pointed to where the staff of the rebel flag crossed over the staff of the national flag. "Put that one behind. The Union won."

Adams erased the crossing, and with quick strokes corrected the sketch.

"Now down here at the bottom, between the flag staffs, put 1901, with my initials on the left, and yours on the right. That will immortalize your freedom from hatred, Son."

The date added, Roosevelt sat staring at the paper. "How soon can I have the medals?"

Adams said, "The standard answer, Sir, is six months."

The president snorted. "Six months, my foot. I'll give your department two weeks. I want four medals, three in bronze and one in gold. The bronze copies are to be simple medallions, and the gold one is to hang on a ribbon, vertical stripes, red, white and blue. Stamp those four, and then destroy the dies. No, make that four bronze. Keep one for yourself. I won't make a public presentation to you. Yours will be a private celebration between us. This will give honor where honor is due for service to the nation, but the image will fade into the past along with the animosity. That's all, Adams. Thank you. Tell your boss I said expedite. I want those ready in two weeks or less."

Roosevelt grabbed a pencil and paper, and sat thinking. He wrote, *Kindly schedule my private train to Chicago in two weeks. Arrange a venue where I can make a speech and a presentation. Invite the usual dignitaries, press, and a couple of people I want on the platform with me. I want the publisher of this magazine, Bub Abbott, and Tobias Mason. Mason is a reporter, so the local newspaper editor can assign him to report on the event.*

He slipped the paper inside the cover of the magazine, and summoned an intern. "Please take this to my secretary. No response needed."

Toby was summoned to the office of his editor. "I'm to cover the event for the president of the country? Why me?"

"Because I want you to cover it. Eight o'clock tonight."

"All right, Sir. I'll do my best."

The venue was crowded. Toby presented his press credentials at the security check.

"Mason? Come with me, if you please." The uniformed officer led Toby to a door where a small group gathered, waiting.

Toby recognized his agent. "Mister Abbott! What are you doing here?"

Abbott shrugged. "Nobody refuses an invitation from the president, Toby."

An hour later, Toby stood outside the hall, a dazed expression on his face. Abbott approached him and said, "The highest levels, Toby. I told you it was that good. I had no idea it would lead to this, though. You, me, your publisher, all three of us get medals because the president thinks we did something great for the country. You did it, Son. What a research stunt that was. Lying on the battlefield in the darkness to feel what those two wounded men felt. I'm proud of your accomplishment, but I'm humbled by the president's words of praise that spilled over onto me." He grasped Toby's hand. "I'm going to have to think this through. Thank you, and thank Sam Clemens for sending you. Bring me an Americana story, Toby. I need to come down to Earth after this evening."

Toby smiled. "I'm working on one, but it is not finished yet." The two men parted, each walking slowly into the evening, thinking.

Headlines rolled across the country next morning. *TOBIAS MASON AWARDED PRESIDENTIAL MEDAL OF MERIT.* Toby's notepad had been blank. His editor was in attendance, and had written what he knew Toby could not.

WHISTLE PIG

CHAPTER SEVENTEEN

Blackwell carried Ginny's grip from the train into the Portland station. She walked beside him as he hurried, hoping to catch a streetcar to Hiram's home. Suddenly he stopped and stared. "Ginny! Look at that headline!"

The banner across the top of the newspaper read, *TOBIAS MASON AWARDED PRESIDENTIAL MEDAL OF MERIT.*

"Ginny, I told you you'd be hearing of him, but I had no idea!"

Ginny scanned the newsstand. Paper after paper bore the same news of Toby, but not one had a picture of him. She was still groping in the dark. What did he look like now? How would she know him? How could she love a faceless name?

Blackwell bought a paper, and they hurried to catch the car. They boarded just as it began to move. "Just made it, Girl. But it's too dark to read this. Maybe Hiram has a paper."

Ginny murmured, "They did not include a picture of him. I still don't know what he looks like. How will I know him?"

"His eyes will not change, Ginny. His eyes."

At home, Ginny scanned the story under the headline. The president had been impressed with Toby's story. He had written the story from his father's letter to her father. "He did it! I told him to write that story. He did! And look what it got him! The president of the country gave him a medal!" Tears blurred her vision, so the story swam. "I'm so proud of him! I'm so glad!"

Uncle Hiram asked, "Then why the tears, Ginny?"

Blackwell answered for her. "Its because she's a girl, Hiram." Then he whispered, "A girl in love! I heard her holler from the pond down south. She called, 'I love you, Toby Mason!' She does not know I was on the porch and heard her. One day, I hope those two meet again. Toby will be a lucky man."

A week later, Ginny found a package beside her plate at the dinner table. Uncle Hiram said, "You have a message from Chicago, Ginny. We will wait dinner while you open it. I am certain it cannot wait. Or perhaps it is you who cannot wait. Go ahead."

Ginny laughed. "Oh, come, now. You are just as curious as I am, if you dare to admit it!"

"I confess, Girl. Open it up. If that is a letter, it can wait until later. We'd starve before you got through that!"

Ginny untied the string that bound the package, and pulled the wrapper open. Their eyes fell on the bold title on the magazine cover: *SHILOH.*

Ginny gasped. "He sent me his article! Wait. It says it was by Garrett James, not Toby Mason."

"Honey, he probably does the same thing you do, and writes under an assumed name."

Ginny giggled. "That's it. He used names to honor both of our fathers. He took my father's last name as his first name, and his father's first name as his last name. What a dear thing for him to do. That could almost make me love him."

Uncle Hiram chuckled. "I heard that you already declared you do love him, Girl."

Ginny blushed. "And who told you such a tale as that?"

"Well, it might have been a little blackbird." He winked across the table at Ginny. "Blackwell was on the porch when you hollered, 'I love you, Toby Mason!' He said you were at the pond down south."

Ginny smiled. "So I did. And I meant it, too. I just realized it, and had to let him know. Maybe the willows will tell him, if he ever visits our valley.

That reminds me of a thought I had while I was there. Could you check with Mister Blackwell to see if I could get the old school house? The roof is falling in. If I could buy it for a song, I would be willing to sing, just so I could fix it up."

"Good dodge, Ginny. But I won't follow that red herring. How can you love Toby, after all these years, when he is so far away?"

"He said I could. I asked him before we left the valley, and he said I could if I wanted to. Then he kissed me."

"Ginny, that was when you were children. You were only eight."

"Love grows up, though."

"You loved what he was. You do not know what he is now."

"Let me love him, Uncle Hiram. I'll find out what he is now when I read this." She patted the magazine.

"Let's eat, and then you can read your article."

When dinner was over and the dishes cleared away, Ginny opened the magazine and discovered a clipping from the Chicago newspaper, and a letter from Toby.

Ginny fluttered her hands. "I don't know which to read first!"

"Well, he put the package so you would see the magazine first, the article from the paper second, and the letter third. There's your order, Ginny. Read the magazine first, then let me read it while you read the other two things."

Before she turned the first page, Ginny was wracked by sobs. Her hand reached across toward Uncle Hiram, clutching at the air. He pulled a handkerchief out of his pocket, and placed it in her groping hand. The next several minutes were spent alternately reading and blotting her eyes. When she finished, she pushed the magazine across to her waiting uncle. It was not long before his hand was reaching across the table. It was a moist handkerchief she placed in his palm.

"We know exactly what he is now, Ginny. Only a true man could write that. He is a man of character, a man of honor."

"When he kissed me, he said it was a promise."

Hiram winked. "That seals it, then. You have my permission to love the man he is, not just the boy he was. Now, the newspaper. We know the headline. What did they say about him in Chicago?"

"They called him a local boy. They can't have him. He's ours." Ginny read on. "They said it was a surprise to him. That the president said his was the greatest message of reconciliation he had seen, and that he hoped it would be the balm that would heal the wounds left in society by the war.

That the president shook hands with Toby, and then hugged him in front of a cheering crowd. The president said he knew personally of one man who had been freed from what he called hand-me-down hatred and that he hoped that man's tribe would increase."

Uncle Hiram nodded. "Now, take your letter up to your room and read it. You can share what you feel is shareable later. I'm going to savor the thought that Toby spent time under this roof. It is a real blessing to know him, or know of him. Thank you, Ginny. He's a man I would like to get to know better."

Ginny reached for the hanky again. "You do not know how earnestly I want that opportunity for you!"

Toby's letter was mostly a mundane account of his existence in the big city. On the second page, he spoke of how he had chosen his pen name to honor both fathers, both soldiers whose story made the article possible. He then told of his conversation with Samuel Clemens, and the trip to Shiloh to live what the soldiers had lived. Ginny shook her head. "He ate hard tack, and lay on the ground where they had fallen wounded. That's how he knew."

It was toward the bottom of the second page that Ginny's eyes opened wide. *'Ginny, I kissed you long ago. I told you it was a promise. If I ever find you, may I kiss you again? I told you once that you could love me if you wanted to. May*

I love you, Ginny? You said there were many girls here in Chicago. There are, but I have not seen one who really loves and honors Jesus, and lives that way consistently.

Ginny drew a shuddering breath. Love had grown up.

∧ ∧ ∧

"Pa, I'm going west. I'm going to visit Millie, and the valley. I have a project I want to do on the hillside across from the house. I'll be back next month."

George Mason smiled at the mature confidence of his nephew who was now his son. "You go. Whatever is buzzing in that skull of yours is a work of honor, and I endorse it. No! Don't tell me what it is. Just go and get it finished. While you are there, see if you can find a story seed or two. Then come back here and write.

"But before you go, there are a few things I want to explain to you. Millie's trust is fully funded, and will pay her until she...no longer needs it. I lost a lot of resources back in the financial panic from 1893 to 1897. I made sure my clients did not lose their livelihoods. If anything happens to me, Janet gets this house and a fund to maintain it, and one to keep her. My partners will buy out my share of the business. If anything happens to both of us, the house and the funds revert to you as my heir. You are the last of the Mason family, unless you find a girl who will have you, and give you a son or two. I did not lose everything, so if you so choose, you will be free to live as a starving writer. But, with that award and the endorsement of Sam Clemens, I think you'll do all right.

"By the way, did I ever tell you how proud of you I am?"

"You did, Pa. About forty-'leven times. But keep on doing it. I forget!"

They both laughed.

"Go get your stuff together, and I'll go with you to the train, Son."

The west-bound train had rattled and clattered south from Chicago, and then headed for the Pacific Ocean. It left the prairie, and plunged into the desert. It slowed, and crept across a repaired trestle. Below, at the bottom of the arroyo, broken freight cars and an engine lay half-buried by flash floods. Later, the engine stopped at a water tank for a refill. Across the tracks, the passengers could see a rustic collection of buildings, bleached by the desert sun. The conductor called, "Water stop, one hour. Hotel serves hot meals and warm lemonade. Jackrabbit stew and biscuits, take it or leave it. One hour, folks, or get left behind!"

Toby chuckled. "Jackrabbit stew. Pa said that's what Mother had to eat for two weeks. Jackrabbit stew and biscuits. It's a wonder they have any of those big-eared hoppers left!" He ate it, and was back aboard waiting when the engine puffed and hissed to life and motion.

At San Francisco, he changed trains and headed north toward Oregon. At Salem, he rented a buggy and drove out to the valley and pulled up to the house. Jackson saw him coming, and came to take the horse.

"He's mine for about a month, Jackson. Take good care of him!"

Jackson stared, then said, "Mister Toby! I didn't know you at first. My, what a man you've become!"

Millie heard the commotion, and came out on the porch. "Why, bless my soul, it's Mister Toby! Get up here, young man, and get yourself a hug!" She gave him a kiss on the cheek as a bonus. "Ginny was here about three months ago. She did not stay long enough, if you ask me. First time I've seen her since she was this little! My, has she ever grown into a lovely lady. She slept in your room. Shall I fix the guest room for you, or do you want to sleep where she did?"

"Well, Millie, I'm all right with it as long as she wore night clothes."

Millie winked. "I can't guarantee that, Toby."

Toby grinned. "I'll sleep there anyway. Did she swim in the pond?"

Millie nodded. "She did, but I never saw any swim clothes drying."

Toby pretended to gasp. "Well! I never..."

Millie winked at him. "That's not what I heard, Toby." They both laughed. "I'll tell you what I heard from the pond, though. She was down there swimming, and I was out by the garden when she hollered, 'I love you, Toby Mason!' Just like that." Millie clapped her hand over her mouth.

"That's all right, Millie. The willows would have told me if you hadn't. Or the ground squirrels. They talk a lot."

Next morning, Toby told Millie, "I'm going over to the church to look around. Is it locked? I don't recall that it ever was."

"No, Toby, and it still is not. Preacher John went to glory, and there hasn't been any preaching there since. He's buried over by Ginny's folks, along with Louise Howard. The workers are few these days, Toby. The Word of God is scarce."

"God will change that, Millie. He does His own gleaning. I'll go look around, and remember. I'll visit Preacher John, too. I want to visit those graves."

Toby went to his room and rummaged in his

bag. He pulled out a hammer and chisel, a pencil and a square box. At the church, he found a stick of fire wood Preacher John had left beside the wood stove. "Just right. About two inches across. That should do." He headed for the graves.

Toby pulled the bronze medallion from the box, and on Edward Garrett's stone, he traced around it with his pencil. With the hammer and chisel, he began the slow task of chipping out a recess in the stone. With heavy blows, the chisel powdered the middle of the circle. Toby alternately hammered and blew away the powdered stone. Then he gradually expanded the socket, easing the chisel's corner ever closer to the pencil mark. The afternoon sun was sinking toward the horizon when he took the stick, placed the medallion over the socket, and with three blows from the hammer he seated the bronze into the stone. He blew the dust of the powdered stone away and stood looking at the Medal of Merit centered over the name of Edward Garrett. "That's for you, Ginny. And for my brother in Christ. I've honored you as I've honored your father." He stood back and saluted the fallen soldier. "And now, if only your daughter would have me, the reconciliation would see the next generation. I'll take your silence as consent, Sir. In Christ, you already have your reward."

Toby returned to the house just as the sun was sitting on the horizon. Supper was spreading it's aroma through the kitchen and dining room. "You always perfume the house to tempt a hungry man, Millie. But I only see one place setting. While I'm here, I want you and Jackson to join me at the table. You are not servants to dine separately. Humor me in that if you would, Millie. I can't talk to a fork and spoon."

When he returned from his room, there were three places set at the table. Conversation filled in the gaps of the last eleven years. The land between the valley and Salem had been filling up with incoming settlers. There was a new and bigger school down the valley, but it seemed someone had bought the old school for a song. Repairs to the roof were already ongoing.

Toby said, "I'm glad. If nothing else, it can be a community center. Folks can get to know each other. Kids can have a place for activities. I wonder who bought it?"

Millie shook her head. "I have not been able to find out. Somebody in Portland, I heard."

Toby spent the next day at the church. He swept and dusted, straightened the chairs and filled the wood box. He shoveled out the ashes that choked the stove, and filled the lamps with oil. Finally, he approached the door to Preacher John's room. The first thing he saw was an open box of hymnals. "Preacher John must have bought these himself. We only sang the ones we all knew."

Toby took the songbooks, and spread them among the chairs. There was a large one bound with rings which he placed on the piano. "That is new, too. I wonder if anybody plays?"

Back in the room, Toby looked at the paper

on the desk. There he saw the passage Preacher John had been preparing for his next Sunday. **Heb 6:17-20 Wherein God, willing more abundantly to shew unto the heirs of promise the immutability of his counsel, confirmed it by an oath: That by two immutable things, in which it was impossible for God to lie, we might have a strong consolation, <u>who have fled for refuge to lay hold upon the hope set before us</u>: Which hope we have as an anchor of the soul, both sure and steadfast, and which entereth into that within the veil; Whither the forerunner is for us entered, even Jesus, made an high priest for ever after the order of Melchisedec.**

Preacher John had underlined the *fled for refuge* part and penciled in *Rock of Ages*. The thoughts were already whirling in Toby's head. "I'll do this when I come back here. I'll work on the exposition of that passage. I'll do it for Preacher John. We'll sing *Rock of Ages* for Ginny.

Toby spent the rest of his time gathering notes for writing. He spent afternoons in the pond, leaving his clothes in a heap on the boulder. He tried to picture Ginny swimming beside him, but she was only a blank form, featureless and uninviting. One afternoon, he called out, "I love you, Ginny Garrett!" He thought, "You willows can tell her if she ever comes back here."

As his time in the valley wound down to a close, Toby spent three afternoons seated on his boulder at the head of the pond. His pencil sometimes flew across the pages of his notepad, and sometimes hovered motionless in the air. He felt Ginny's nearness as he wrote. He heard the splashing as she swam through his memory. On his paper he wrote *The Pond*.

WHISTLE PIG

CHAPTER EIGHTEEN

Joseph stood in the parlor doorway. "A gentleman to see you, Sir. He sent this card."

Taking the card, Hiram read, *Samuel L. Clemens*. "Good heavens! He's here?"

Joseph nodded.

"Well, show him in, Joseph, show him in!"

When Joseph turned to receive the late evening guest, Hiram said, "Ginny, it's Sam Clemens. I'm astonished. I do not know the man. I've never met him. What might he want here?"

The bushy-haired man at the parlor door said, "Money. Always give them money, and they will go away."

Through the general laughter, Joseph announced, "Mister Samuel Clemens, Sir." To Clemens, he said, "This gentleman is Hiram Smith, and the girl is his niece, Virginia Garrett."

Clemens looked from Hiram to Ginny. "I must have the wrong house. I'm not looking for either one of you. I came all the way from Connecticut looking for a writer of magazine articles named Virgil Garrison. Pah! I've wasted my time and money. Good evening to you. You will pardon the intrusion. That's an order." He turned to leave.

Hiram roared with laughter. "Hold on, there, you old rascal! Get back here. You have found your writer!"

Clemens stuck his head around the door jamb. "You? I expected someone a bit more youthful. You are too long in the tooth to write what I've been reading. Where's Garrison?"

Hiram bowed toward Ginny. "She's right here, Mister Clemens. Virginia Garrett is a bit bashful, and writes under a pseudonym. Like you do, Mark Twain."

Clemens stepped into the parlor.

Hiram said, "Mark Twain, meet Virgil Garrison."

Ginny extended her hand, and Clemens gingerly took her fingertips. "I won't squeeze, them, Miss." Instead, he raised her hand and kissed them. His bushy mustache tickled her knuckles.

"Très galant, monsieur."

"Great Scott! What happened to the Ozarks?"

"Sorry, Mister Clemens. Ah jes' cain't never git it right, no how."

"That's better, Miss Virginia. Now, by all means sit down, Girl. Or do I have to stand here all evening?"

Ginny giggled, and seated herself beside Hiram. "Take that chair, Mister Clemens. It's comfortable."

"Yes, and it has arms so I can hoist my old bones out of it when it's time to go. I'll leave before you throw me out. Promise."

The old man sat gazing at the young girl. "I read your school house article. Reminded me of myself and my writing. I could feel your wealth of poverty, Miss Virginia. I burned with shame when that young rapscallion lifted your dress. I pummeled that other boy with congratulations when he thrashed the one who uncovered your...nakedness. Miss Virginia, I congratulate you. You portray life in its reality without being crass.

"I reveled in your valley article. I confess I went out and tried to talk to the squirrels. They did not like what I said. They would not talk back. But it took me back to my early days. I relived things I had forgotten. You have that gift.

"I came all the way out here to ask what's next. There always has to be a next. Don't ever let your pencil or your mind get lazy. What are you writing now?"

Ginny blushed. "I hesitate to show you, because I have not decided that I should submit it. I guess you'd call it Americana. I...All right, I'll get it. You might have some insight that could help me decide."

When she returned, she handed Sam Clemens *THE POND*.

Ginny waited anxiously as Clemens read page after page. His stern face softened as he read. When he finished, he read it again, pausing often to sit with his eyes closed. Finally, he looked Ginny's way. "Young lady, I'm going to tell you the same thing I told a young fellow back east. Don't touch it. Get it to your agent as it is. I wish I had written this. I said the same thing to a lad who wrote a recent article entitled *SHILOH*. Made a little noise in the newspapers. You have the same touch on the heart of humanity. This has a universal portrayal of innocence and enjoyment. Send it in."

Ginny's face showed her amazement. "The one who wrote *SHILOH* is the boy you congratulated for standing up for me at the school."

Clemens nodded. "He would. I knew the girl was you, but I did not know the boy was the lad who showed me his feeble efforts at writing that story. I told him to go to Shiloh. I told him his writing was dead, and he should either make it alive or bury it. I wish I could get the two of you together, and spend a summer with you. I admire your writing, Miss Virginia. That's what I came to say." Clemens lurched up from the chair. "And now, if you will excuse me, it's time for an old man to find his pillow. I'll show myself out." He had been busy scribbling as he talked. Before he left, he handed Ginny a scrap of paper.

Opening it she read: *Keep away from people who try to belittle your ambitions, Ginny. Small people always do that. But the really great make you feel that you, too, can become great. Those magazine articles are a scattering of little seeds that people swallow whole, and then the things take root in the mind, and blossom into something wonderful. Write on! You were bare in the pond, but in your stories, you lay bare your soul. This old man thanks you.*

Ginny handed the paper to Uncle Hiram, who sat wondering at what had just occurred. He read the note, and said, "Ginny, that is high praise from one who is stingy with it. Treasure it."

Ginny looked at her manuscript. At the top, she saw a penciled note: *This is perfect – Sam Clemens*

"He autographed it! Now I don't want to send it in. I want it for a memory!"

"Type another copy, Ginny. You might take it to Nobles personally. You can show him the copy Clemens signed, and submit the other copy. On the other hand, you could just send it. Blackwell isn't available to go south with you. You outgrew a governess, and that rascal Woodruff wanted Pete for a wife, so she's gone these two years." Hiram sat thinking. "I could go. I haven't seen Nobles in years. We write, but I'd rather sit and chat face to face. Let's plan on that, Ginny. I can't throw anybody over a rail, but I can scowl and look intimidating. We will go. When would you like to head south, Ginny?"

"Let's go in two weeks. I can send a telegram to Mister Nobles to set up an appointment. I have a couple of questions for him anyway. But, Uncle Hiram! Samuel Clemens has been following my writing! I can't believe it!"

Hiram squeezed her hand. "Don't forget, Honey, that Sam Clemens is a friend of Harold Nobles. He might even get advance notice that a new one is coming out!"

Ginny smiled. "I wish Mister Nobles would give Toby word when my articles are published. I have not seen any indication he even knows about them."

"Toby will know. He may not have time for magazines. Or, he may not read the ones that buy your articles. Probably so busy squiring girls around town that he can't take time for reading."

Ginny giggled, and shook her head. "No, Uncle Hiram, he said there are lots of girls in Chicago, but they put on piety for Sunday, and take it off for the rest of the week. In his letter, he asked if he could love me. I think he might. Other girls don't rate with him."

"Well, Ginny, Sam Clemens had good things to say about him, and that man does not bestow his good opinion lightly or liberally. You have my blessing to give Toby a kiss."

"I already did. And he kissed me. A few times. I can't wait for him to take up where he left off."

"I see. So it is only a couple thousand miles keeping you apart, then?"

Ginny shook her head and sighed. "I suppose. That, and different lives. We might have just grown apart."

"Ginny, this is naughty. I'm warning you in advance, but I'm going to say it anyway. When you see him again, if he kisses you, don't let it be just a peck and run. Reach up and hold his head. Run your fingers through his hair, hold on and make sure that kiss is a good long one. Baby kisses don't say much. Make sure he knows you are all grown up."

"Uncle Hiram!"

"I warned you. You may be shocked now, but do what I tell you, Ginny. He'll know you are no longer that unformed little girl he taught to swim."

The two checked in at the hotel in San Francisco, and met Harold Nobles in the dining room. After dinner, Ginny handed Nobles the manuscript.

"Sam liked it, did he? Can't be any good, then. Sam Clemens is no judge of good writing." Nobles winked at Hiram.

"You don't want it?" Disappointment flavored Ginny's question.

"Sarcasm, my girl. Sarcasm. That was a slight on my good friend Sam Clemens. No. Your article is perfect, as Clemens said. It exceeds your previous submissions, and they were superb. Here. You keep the copy Sam signed. I'll take this other one, if you don't mind."

Ginny smiled, and Hiram heard relief in her words when she said, "Oh, I thank you. I've been holding that one, trying to decide whether to submit it. I wrote it on the train the first time I met you."

Nobles winced. "That was a difficult trip for you, Ginny. No such incidents this time, we trust."

Ginny closed her eyes and shook her head. "I pray nothing like that happens ever again!"

∧ ∧ ∧

Toby struggled with his notes and his rough

draft of *THE POND* from Oregon all the way to Chicago. He had been to the valley. He swam in the pond, but as he wrote, somehow the article remained flat and lifeless. It had the basic story, but there had to be something more. His story lacked... He pondered the issue. It lacked heart.

His quandary continued once he reached home in Chicago. He paced. He read and reread his notes. The pencil snapped in half between his fingers. "It does not only lack heart, it lacks focus. Something that has universal appeal. It can't just be swimming naked. What underlies the enjoyment? Where is it headed?"

He grabbed the pointed half of the broken pencil, and scrawled across the top of his notes: *THE SEEDS OF LOVE.*

Ginny had said of Auntie Gert, "She didn't love them." But the focus came next: *KIN I LOVE YOU, TOBY?* And he had answered: *I GUESS, IF YOU WANT TO.* The focus was not on bare bodies in the pond, but on the deep human need to love and be loved that was laid bare in those words. He had the theme.

Line after line, page by page, Toby interwove the shared swimming with the heart need each struggled to have satisfied. Ginny's mother loved her, but with her few remaining days and limited resources, the girl's love need was precariously positioned. With Toby's mother, the problem was misdirected love. Hers was a self love focused on an artificial status. Toby was left empty.

It was thus that, innocent of clothes and of shame, the seeds of love were scattered in their days. They were seeds that would germinate over the years, watered by longing thoughts that groped across the chasm of time and distance.

Toby's pencil paused, then hovered over the page. He did not know the end of the story. "I could make it up, and nobody would know the difference. Happily ever after and all. But that would be not only maudlin, but a lie. It would be better to leave us both wondering and wanting. I'll do that, and see what Mister Abbott thinks. I won't know the end until I find Ginny, if I ever do. I know where she lives, but our encounter would have to be natural. The seeds cannot be forced. Ginny said she would pray that Jesus would bring us back together. I will, too. The Lord has His own purposes, His own timing, and His own ways. I'll wait on Him."

Toby decided to let the pond story rest, and turned to the message he planned to take to the valley. For an hour, his pencil was poised over a blank paper. Then, thumbing through his Bible, his eyes focused on the words of the apostle Paul. *This one thing I do...*

"That's the trouble. I can work up the article, or I can work up the message. I'll do the message once the article is in Abbott's hands. So for tonight, I'll sleep on the article. Tomorrow I'll try to get it typed. I cannot depend on Judy for that."

By noon the next day, the number of wadded and discarded pages far outnumbered the finished pages of the story. However, it was done. He decided that Monday he would take it to Mister Abbott. It had typing errors, but Judy would have to make copies for distribution anyway, so he did not bother to retype the document. He could not really call it a manuscript, because that indicated it was written longhand. "Common usage. If everybody makes the same mistake, then it is accepted as right. Like in Israel. Every man did that which was right in his own eyes. But God does not see it that way. I need some wisdom."

Downstairs, he sat with George Mason. "Pa, I need some counsel. Wise counsel. You are elected."

"I'll try, Son. What is the trouble?"

"Me, I guess. I've fulfilled my obligation to Mister Abbott with this story. I'll take it to him Monday. But what then? I visited Millie at the house in the valley when I was out west. Preacher John is dead. Louise Howard is dead. Those were the reapers in that field of the Lord's. I went to the church. Millie says nobody has spoken the Word since Preacher John went home. Here's my trouble. I know the Word. The church here ordained me to share the Word of God.

"While I was in that little church, I found the passage Preacher John was getting ready for the next Sunday. I want to preach that message, in memory of Preacher John. I don't know if anybody would come, but I want to pull the rope and ring the bell to call the valley to hear that message. I know Millie is hungry in spirit, because she told me so. Others may be like sheep without a shepherd. My writing is fine, but it is earthbound. I may well be needed in that little church.

"Here is my dilemma. Part of me hopes that Ginny might be there. If I go, and if I stay there, it would have to be for the glory of the Lord, and not for my wants. Millie told me that Ginny was there three months before I was. I just missed her. All that is a roundabout way of asking you to read this. Overlook the typing errors, and tell me what you think."

When he had read through the story, George sat staring at the china hutch. His eyes traced the shapes of the handles of the tea cups, and the pattern on the teapot. Finally, he looked at Toby.

"Son, you and Ginny are thinly veiled here, even though you were not at all veiled in that pond. But this goes beyond the two of you. You cannot force the seeds of the love of the Lord, or His plans. In that you are correct. If you go there, you will find the reality of the parable of the sower. You'll have all of those kinds of soil, and all of those results. You will meet disappointment and rejection. But, in harmony with your theme, Paul said, 'I planted, Apollos watered, and the Lord gave the increase.' It's the same in gardening and in preaching.

"If you know that at the beginning, you will have the strength and light from the Lord to carry on. If you feel that is your calling, go. Janet and I will not hold you back. We will pray for you. You already have a home there, and Millie and Jackson can do for you. You have enough to keep you, and I know you would not flaunt what you have. View it all as from the Lord. Some day, there will be a dynamo there, and you can add lights to the church, and a furnace. You can add a wing, and put in indoor plumbing. Those are things for physical comfort. But the Word is to nourish the spirit. The other things are worthless if the spirit is perishing.

"When did you think you might go with that message?"

"I was thinking next fall, unless something comes up to take me out west beforehand. But I don't know. I'm just going in circles here. I'm not really doing anything. It is as if the writing was a chapter, or a season, and now the seasons are changing."

George Mason chuckled. "And is the wind from the north, or the south?"

"Well, it is warm, so it must be from the south. But it's circling west, it seems."

"Just like my brother James. He couldn't wait to go west, even with his wounds. I'm not sure what was waiting there for him, unless it was you. I know what you are hoping for. She might end up there. The Lord knows what He is doing." He waved the article in the air. "I think this is fine. I think it is ready for Abbott. Now, go work on that message. The Lord is working in you, and He wants to work through you. That valley may well be your field. The heart need of humanity is universal. Bless you in your ministry, Son."

WHISTLE PIG

CHAPTER NINETEEN

Restlessness caused Ginny to pace through the day, and toss and turn at night. Her article was in the process, and she was not currently shaping another. She had left the pond article in the hands of Mister Nobles and in the hands of the Lord. "I've done well, and yet I'm not satisfied. There has to be something more to life than writing and waiting for money to come in. I get all of the glory, and my Lord gets so little. Why am I not being used to bring glory to Jesus?"

Ginny's mind went to something Millie had said that time she had visited. There was no reaper, no gleaner in the valley since the deaths of Preacher John and Louise Howard. The little church had not gathered since. Her heart was drawn. "But I'm unprepared. I know nothing. How can the Lord use a tool that is not sharp?"

Her agitation was interrupted and heightened by a telegram: *Problem with Pond article stop Must talk stop Come south stop Nobles*

She tapped on the library door, and entered. "Uncle Hiram, I just received this." She handed him the message from her agent. "It must be serious. He wants me in San Francisco."

Hiram frowned. "I can't break away just now, Ginny. You've been there often enough to find your way. Are you comfortable going alone?"

Ginny nodded. "I could do it. And then on the way home, I could stop and see Millie. I've been restless, and the valley seems to be the focus. I don't know why. I feel I should go there."

Chuckling, Hiram said, "Advice from Sam Clemens fits in this case, then. He said, 'If it is your job to eat a frog, do it first thing in the morning. If you have to eat two frogs, eat the biggest one first.' I'll get you a ticket for Wednesday. They can give you the car numbers to the hotel, and then you can be back in Salem by Saturday. Stay a week with Millie, and then your ticket will bring you back here. Wish I could be your escort, but I'm obligated. Will that do, Honey?"

"I think so. I'm not going to be anxious about the story. I'll pack for both places, and let the Lord handle the details at both stops. Just having a direction, I'm at peace. That has to be the Lord's doing."

"Amen, Honey. Run along, now, and get ready. You'll have to be up and running early day after tomorrow."

Ginny rifled through her closet. "I don't really need anything super dressy. I'll meet with Mister Nobles, though. I wore this white linen suit last time. And the time before!" She slid that hanger aside, and pulled out her brown skirt and jacket. "This is presentable, but not formal. I'll wear this..." she pulled out two blouses, one white, and one creamy. "This will give me two outfits." On a whim, she pulled out a skirt and jacket of navy doeskin, and a pale blue blouse. "Just in case there is a dressy occasion. I could wear this to Millie's." From her bureau, she pulled her blue lace cravat. The better clothes she slipped into a folding garment bag, and packed everyday wear in a suitcase. "Black boots and moccasins. I don't need a hat. A scarf will do."

By eight o'clock Wednesday morning, she was seated in the passenger car, ticket in hand. Uncle Hiram had secured a private compartment in the sleeper for her, and the dining car would supply simple fare for her meals. As the train rolled southward through the Willamette Valley, Ginny recognized her wrinkle in the hills. Civilization was expanding toward the mountains on both sides of the big valley, filling the valleys and ridges with farms and small settlements.

In San Francisco, Ginny sat across from Harold Nobles. "I have no idea how they could get two similar manuscripts. I could withdraw mine from consideration. Samuel Clemens urged me to submit it, but I don't need to have it published, Mister Nobles. It is mine though. Here." She reached into her bag. "Do you read shorthand? This is the original I wrote on the way south the first time I came down to meet you."

Nobles shook his head. "No, Ginny, shorthand is not something I learned. Don't withdraw it, though. Not yet. I have a friend working on the thing from the other end. I don't have a copy of the other manuscript, but he has both. Just wait on his work. We will get this figured out. It's funny, though, that the same magazine got both submissions."

Ginny rose to leave. "So there is nothing more to do at this time? Can the rest be handled by mail or telegraph? You've answered my other concerns, and the business side is clear to me now."

"It can. When do you head back home?"

"I can go tonight, if you will not need anything from me. Or, I could buy a few things and go tomorrow. At any rate, I'll be home a week from Sunday."

"That will do, Ginny. I'm certain everything will work out. Don't worry."

"I'm not concerned, Mister Nobles. I'm at peace. It's in the Lord's hands."

As Ginny turned to go, she noticed a young man who, directed by the hostess, headed toward Mister Nobles' table. She nodded a greeting, and he glanced at her as she stepped aside, then out the door. There, she paused, then headed up the stairs. She would get a good night's rest, and tomorrow she would buy a few things for Millie and Jackson, and take the train north.

She had a refreshing bath next morning, and as she ate her breakfast, she composed a mental shopping list.

Ginny checked her bags at the railway station, and they were loaded into the baggage car as she boarded a streetcar and headed out to do her shopping. She had fifteen minutes to spare as she left the streetcar and hurried into the station, crossed the platform and boarded the northbound train. Seated in the passenger car, she felt the train lurch, and start forward. It was still moving slowly along the platform when an athletic young man sprinted down the platform, grabbed the rail and swung aboard the caboose.

∧ ∧ ∧

"I'm headed west, Pa. I'm to meet a man named Harold Nobles in San Francisco. He is a literary agent there. Mister Abbott said there is some question about my last article. Something about plagiarism. He's sending me there to try to get to the bottom of the problem."

That conversation had preceded Toby's packing and departure. Abbott had given him copies of his article and the other one that had raised the issue with the magazine publisher who had received both. He would read both as the train rolled south, and then west. "I'll chat with Nobles, and see what can be done. I suppose I could just withdraw mine, and let the other run."

Once the train had skirted the Sierras, the weather cooled. As it headed toward San Francisco, Toby changed to a sweater. He would go casual instead of formal. At the station, Toby took his suitcase with the portfolio and his folder that held his notes for his message for Sunday, and left his other baggage routed for Salem.

Fog had settled over the area when he stepped off the streetcar and headed into the hotel. He checked in, took his bag to his room, and took out the portfolio he and Nobles would examine. Downstairs, he entered the dining room. To the hostess he said, "I'm to meet a man named Harold Nobles here. Do you know him? Is he here?"

The woman smiled, and pointed. "He is sitting over there, where that young lady just stood up." Toby thanked the hostess, and headed across the room. Nobles looked like a reasonable man, he thought. He nodded a greeting to the young woman, who stepped aside to let him pass. He caught the older man's eye, and extended his hand. Nobles rose, and took the hand, saying, "I'm Harold Nobles."

Toby laid the portfolio on the table. "I'm Toby Mason. Bub Abbott said I should come west to see you about a difficulty that has arisen over an article I wrote." He pulled out a chair, and sat across from Nobles."

"Abbott. I know him. Quite well, actually."

Toby laughed. "You two are very different. He's as smooth as a gravel road."

"Until you get to know him." Nobles chuckled. "Rubbed you the wrong way, did he? He is a rather no-nonsense sort."

Toby nodded. "Mister Nobles, I noticed you keep rather attractive company. Who was that young lady who was leaving as I arrived?"

"She's one of my clients. Writes under the name of Virgil Garrison."

Toby jumped up, and when he whirled toward the door, he sent his chair skittering across the floor. When he reached the door, there was no one in view.

Toby returned and picked up his chair. Seated again, he shook his head. "I crossed the continent to find Virgil Garrison. And she's a girl?"

Nobles nodded. "That's her pen name. She's Virginia Garrett. She hid behind a man's name that came from her own."

"That was Ginny? I haven't seen her in years. I wish I had paid more attention to her. I did not get a good look at her, so I would not recognize her if I saw her again."

He opened the portfolio. "That brings me to the reason I'm here. But I have one answer, sort of. Abbott gave me copies of two articles. I wrote one. The other was submitted by you under the name of Virgil Garrison. The question that has come up is one of plagiarism. Read these. Abbott has highlighted the similarities. Since Ginny wrote this one, the things that are alike are so because we both lived those scenes.

"Here is the challenge. The same magazine received both articles. Obviously, they cannot print both. Read them, and tell me what you think we should do."

Toby turned to watch the door, in case Ginny returned. He waited in vain.

Nobles cleared his throat. "Mister Mason..."

"Toby. You are free to use my name, Sir."

"Toby. I don't think either of you needs to withdraw your submission. You feature the seeds of love. She is focused on childhood innocence. The solution is to submit one of them to a different magazine. I'll contact Abbott. Virginia has been published in the one that has the two articles a few times. These are only submissions. No money has been sent anywhere yet. Abbott can get in touch with the publisher who was next in line. We can explain the similarities, and they will know there is no plagiarism, and can decide on the publication date, so they are not on the newsstand at the same time."

Toby nodded. "I just wish I had known who she was. I'll tell you this. In both articles, she is the girl. I'm the boy. We lived in the same valley, with that pond between our homes. We parted ways. She went to Portland, and I went to Chicago. We've written a couple of times, but I'm afraid we have lost touch. She glanced at me, but did not know me. I glanced at her, but did not know her."

Nobles was thoughtful. "One of you should write that story. I don't know which one. I like your style, and I've done well with her style. Maybe each of you should write it, and Abbott and I could decide which one to submit. Virginia told me she had another story to write, but she said she did not know the ending yet. If you are in that story, Son, don't hesitate to write that ending. I'll add this. She was nearly killed in this very hotel. That lovely girl needs someone who will take care of her. I don't know what she decided. She may have taken tonight's train north. She was not decided between tonight and tomorrow. Are you going back east?"

Toby shook his head. "No. I'm going north, too. I'll catch tomorrow's train. I have a room here for tonight."

Nobles nodded. "Get a good night's sleep, then." This was spoken absentmindedly. Then, as he had been looking at the two manuscripts, he said, "I remember Sam Clemens wrote on Virginia's article. She kept that copy. Ever meet him? If he has things to say, pay attention. He does not spend his words freely."

He handed the papers to Toby, who returned them to his portfolio. As he zipped it closed, Toby said, "It was a pleasure meeting you, Mister Nobles. I will wait to hear from Mister Abbott as to the fate of my story. Thank you for your kind words about Ginny. I'm shocked that she was almost killed."

"Some hired killer clapped a chloroform-soaked rag over her face, and she wilted. He was going to drag her somewhere to kill her, when Virginia's companion sent him to his own death. Most unnerving. The guy landed on his head on the marble floor right out there. Go up to the first landing, and that's where she was, lying unconscious."

It was with knotted stomach that Toby climbed the stairs on the way to his room.

WHISTLE PIG

CHAPTER TWENTY

Toby slept late. As he descended the stairs, he had to resist the urge to step over the prone Ginny he saw in his mind. He closed his eyes, and was not aware he was holding his breath until it released in an audible explosion of air. Somebody had paid to have the girl killed! He shook his head in disbelief, and hurried to the dining room for a late breakfast.

He dawdled over a second cup of coffee, thinking ahead. He pulled out his turnip of a pocket watch and jumped up. He paid his tab, and took the stairs two at a time, then came clattering down with his suitcase. He slapped the key on the counter, and said to the clerk, "Late!" and dashed out the door. He made quite a spectacle dashing through the station. When he reached the platform, he saw the train starting to roll down the track. He sprinted after it, caught the rail and swung onto the caboose platform with his suitcase in hand. The door stood open, and he stepped inside as the brakeman was hanging up his flags.

"Well, young man, you cut things kinda close. Got a ticket?"

Toby nodded, and reached for it.

The brakeman shook his head. "Hold onto it. If you are going through to Oregon, you'll run into the conductor. He's the one to punch that for you."

Toby stuffed the ticket back in his pocket, and said, "I've always wanted to ride in the tail of the train. Do you mind? I have a drawing room in the sleeper car, but is it all right to sit here and take notes? I'm a writer."

"Well, son, if you are writing, you won't be much company."

Toby laughed. "Tell you what. We'll talk, and I'll just take notes. Like Sam Clemens did on the steamboat. Rode at the bridge with the captain. He said he learned a lot about the river that way."

"Sam Clemens?"

"You might recognize him as Mark Twain. That was his pen name."

Understanding flared in the brakeman's face. "Tom Sawyer. That Mark Twain."

Toby nodded, as he set his suitcase under the table, and sat on the seat with his pencil and pad.

"What do you write?"

On the shelf, Toby saw the magazine with SHILOH emblazoned across the cover. He pointed. "That."

Wide eyed, the brakeman said, "You wrote SHILOH?"

"I did. I had to." He explained the background of the story.

The brakeman mused, "My father was at Shiloh. He never said anything except, 'It was bad. Really bad.'" He thought a minute, then said, "Say! You are that kid that got a medal from the president! Let me shake your hand! Nobody will believe who rode north with me!"

Five cars ahead, Ginny pulled the SHILOH magazine out and reread the story. The woman next to her saw it, and said, "Say, that was really a special article. My father was there, and he came home a bitter man. There was a man in our town who had been on the other side. My father hated him. Being secesh, he was shunned by the whole town. But after reading that article, my father hunted him up and bought him dinner at the restaurant. They have been friendly ever since."

Ginny smiled. "That is what Toby would have wanted."

"What do you mean, Toby? Look there. The fellow who wrote that was Garrett James. How do you get Toby out of that?"

"I know Toby. We lived in the same valley.

The two soldiers featured in the article were our fathers. Toby's father was Union, while mine was Confederate. That theme of reconciliation reached your father's heart, and changed it. That is why Toby wrote the story. He took our fathers' names as his pen name. My last name is Garrett. His father was James Mason."

Recognition and fear swept across the woman's face. To cover, she asked, "Wasn't he the boy that received that medal from the president?"

Ginny felt a shiver course through her. "He was. He is. I was never so proud in my life."

The woman hesitated, then asked, "May I read that again?"

Ginny handed her the magazine. Suddenly, the woman lowered the article to her lap. "He talks about being reconciled to God. Why would that be necessary?"

A quick prayer ran through Ginny's mind, "Father, give me the words. Bring the Scriptures to my mind. And please open her understanding."

"It's because we all either are or were enemies of God. He created us to glorify Himself, and we are set on getting all the glory for ourselves. The Lord tells us, **'For all have sinned, and come short of the glory of God.'** He demands perfection. We cannot achieve that. We need Him to change us."

The woman shook her head. "Honey, you

don't have to tell me anything about sin. I carry that burden inside me."

Ginny sighed. "Ma'am, it is more than the burden you carry. It is the consequences as well."

"And that, my dear, is what frightens me."

"It should. The Lord says in His Word, **'Wherefore, as by one man sin entered into the world, and death by sin; and so death passed upon all men, for that all have sinned.'** We are born with that tendency to rebel against God and what is right. We want what we see going on around us. It looks like pleasure, but it poisons us. That death that we received is not just for here and now. My parents died, but they knew and loved Jesus. Those who don't will die spiritually as well, and be separated from God forever.

"The Bible describes what we are like when we are enemies of God. It says, **'And you hath he quickened, who were dead in trespasses and sins; wherein in time past ye walked according to the course of this world, according to the prince of the power of the air, the spirit that now worketh in the children of disobedience: among whom also we all had our conversation in times past in the lusts of our flesh, fulfilling the desires of the flesh and of the mind; and were by nature the children of wrath, even as others.'"**

The woman next to Ginny sighed. "That is exactly where I am. Is there no hope?"

Ginny smiled at the woman. "There is. We sin. All of us. We work hard to earn what God has promised for those who reject Jesus. The Lord shows us the way of hope. He says,'**For the wages of sin is death; but the gift of God is eternal life through Jesus Christ our Lord.'** Jesus is our only hope. God's message of hope is contained in one passage of Scripture: '**For God so loved the world, that he gave his only begotten Son, that whosoever believeth in him should not perish, but have everlasting life. For God sent not his Son into the world to condemn the world; but that the world through him might be saved. He that believeth on him is not condemned: but he that believeth not is condemned already, because he hath not believed in the name of the only begotten Son of God.'** That is God's message of grace. His only demand is that we believe what He has said, and receive what He offers us."

"But I thought we were all part of God's family, and He would welcome us all when we die. Isn't God our Heavenly Father?"

"There are some who like to tell us that, but God says differently. God sent Jesus as His message of salvation. Jesus was rejected. The Bible tells us, '**He came unto his own, and his own received him not. But as many as received him, to them gave he power to become the sons of God, even to them that believe on his name: which were born, not of blood, nor of the will of the flesh, nor of the will of man,** but of God.' For those who are not born of God, into His family, there is a different message. There were very religious people who rejected Jesus. He told them, **'Ye are of your father the devil, and the lusts of your father ye will do. He was a murderer from the beginning, and abode not in the truth, because there is no truth in him. When he speaketh a lie, he speaketh of his own: for he is a liar, and the father of it.'** As enemies of God, we sin, because we follow our spiritual father, the devil. We cannot honor God, until He draws us to His Son, Jesus Christ. But that is what God is doing. By His Holy Spirit, His Word, and the testimony of those who are His, He draws us. The Bible says, **'But God, who is rich in mercy, for his great love wherewith he loved us, even when we were dead in sins, hath quickened us together with Christ, (by grace ye are saved) and hath raised us up together, and made us sit together in heavenly places in Christ Jesus.'"**

The woman cried, "I want that, Girl! Oh, how I want that!"

Ginny prayed silently, "Show her the way, Father. Draw her. Help her to embrace the Savior!" To the woman, she said, "Jesus took your sins on Himself, and carried them to the cross where He died. The wrath of God against your sins fell on Jesus. He offers newness of life here, and eternal life hereafter. The Bible says, **'Herein is love, not that we loved God, but that he loved us, and sent his Son to be the propitiation for our sins.'** That word, propitiation means God's offended holiness is satisfied, and the judgment against our sins has been paid in full. Now we have hope. Now, we do not face condemnation when we see God. Instead, as the Bible says, **'Blessed be the God and Father of our Lord Jesus Christ, who hath blessed us with all spiritual blessings in heavenly places in Christ: according as he hath chosen us in him before the foundation of the world, that we should be holy and without blame before him in love: having predestinated us unto the adoption of children by Jesus Christ to himself, according to the good pleasure of his will, to the praise of the glory of his grace, wherein he hath made us accepted in the beloved.'"**

The weeping woman asked, "But how can that be mine? You don't know me, or my past."

Ginny reached over and touched the woman's shoulder. "There is only one way it can be yours. The Bible says, **'That if thou shalt confess with thy mouth the Lord Jesus, and shalt believe in thine heart that God hath raised him from the dead, thou shalt be saved. For with the heart man believeth unto righteousness; and with the mouth confession is made unto salvation.'** The transaction is between you and God. Give Him your brokenness, and be made whole. Tell Him you believe, then tell others what God has done for you. Get together with other believers, and grow in grace and the knowledge of our Lord and Savior Jesus Christ.

"You are right. I know nothing about you,

but God knows all about you, and loves you anyway. I don't even know your name. Tell me your first name, and I will pray for you, dear one."

"No, I suppose three years where I have been have changed my appearance, Ginny. I'm Gertrude. I'm your father's cousin. I tried to have you killed. Can you ever forgive me?"

Ginny stared at the prison pallor and deep lines that marred her aunt's face. "I forgave you long ago. I could not carry the load of hatred and anger. It paralyzed me and kept me from truly living. You are forgiven, Auntie Gert."

"I'm on my way to ask Hiram to forgive me as well."

Ginny gathered the woman into an embrace. "I'll pray for you, Auntie. Trust Jesus."

Five cars back, Toby went over his notes for his message.

The brakeman was in and out of the caboose each time it stopped at a water tank or village platform. The sun was setting as the Sierra Madre Mountains swung toward the Trinities. The brakeman asked, "Hungry? The conductor is coming to take my order. You can eat here just as well."

Toby came up to the surface enough to mumble, "That would be great. Order me whatever you are having."

As the sun slipped behind the Trinity Mountains, the brakeman lit the lamps. Toby sighed, and gathered his papers.

"What are you studying there?"

Toby stood and stretched. "I'm planning to preach at a little church out of Salem come Sunday. I don't think anybody has brought the Word since Preacher John died."

"Preacher John is gone? He led me to the Lord!"

Toby grinned. "Me, too. Wasn't he a wonderful man? So humble, and such a big heart!"

"He was. And talk about humble! Nobody ever knew he was once a professor of Bible at a large school back east!"

"Why did he leave?"

"He said they did not believe the Bible. They wanted him to teach human goodness and wisdom. He came to where people were hungry for God's truth, not the worthless husks of philosophy."

Toby chuckled. "I was at his church when I was little. I went back there after he died. On his desk, I found the passage he was going to use the next Sunday. I'm going to use that, not that I will preach the sermon he was going to preach. But, it will be the Word of God, and it will be the gospel of salvation by grace. That was always his message. I don't know if anyone will show up after all of these years, but I am going to ring the bell, and wait. I don't care how many come. If I preach to one, it will be because God wants that one to hear the Word. It may draw that one to Christ, or encourage that one in the Lord. God's Word will accomplish His purpose. I will only be a tool in the hand of the Heavenly Workman."

The brakeman smiled, and slapped Toby on the back. "Son, that is the very attitude Preacher John had every time he spoke. He followed in the footsteps of the Master. You follow where He led, and the Lord will glorify Himself in you."

After eating in the caboose, Toby headed for his drawing room in the sleeper car. "If you don't mind, I'll come back here in the morning. Even with the rhythm of the rails, this is a good place to study."

"Come on back. Breakfast arrives at eight o'clock. I'll order yours."

Toby was asleep when Ginny entered the sleeper car, and retired to her own drawing room. She awoke at nine o'clock, with the sunshine streaming through the window curtain. She dressed, packed her bag, and headed for the dining car for a late breakfast. All that was left was a cup of coffee and two sweet rolls. "I'll get fat, but if that is all there is, I'll eat it."

The train pulled into Salem Saturday afternoon. Toby had his suitcase in hand, and strode across the platform and through the station while Ginny was waiting by the baggage car. Toby left the livery, his rented buggy headed for the valley and the house on the hill.

When Ginny finally got her bags she headed for the hotel. "I'll stay tonight, and surprise Millie tomorrow. I'll sure enjoy a bath!"

Next morning, Ginny pondered her wardrobe. It was Sunday, after all, and Millie was a very special friend. She put on the blue outfit. Breakfast had been much more abundant and nourishing than sweet rolls.

At the livery, she rented a buggy, and headed for the valley.

Morning at the house on the hill was busy. Millie had been surprised when Toby knocked and let himself in. He had shared his plan, and had told Millie, "Don't you give me away tomorrow. I doubt anyone but you might be there, and I suppose that if there is anybody else, people won't know me. But just in case, mum's the word. I'll sneak it in on my introduction. And no talking about that medal, you hear?"

Toby gathered his papers. He had music for a new Fanny Crosby hymn that would go perfectly with his message. He headed for the church. "Listen for the bell, Millie! I'm going to pull that rope until the rafters shake!"

He did just that. He had swept and dusted when he arrived. The hymnals were all still in place. The bell bearings had screeched and squealed as the music of the bell called the valley dwellers to worship. He rang it early to give the surprised residents time to get ready. He went to the front door, and saw dust trailing behind a couple of buggies on the road. Down the valley, he saw scattered walkers headed his way. "Praise the Lord! They must be hungry. Feed them in spite of my stumbling efforts, Lord!"

As Ginny approached the house on the hill, she saw buggies heading for the church. Others were already there. Curious, and hungry for the Word herself, she drove past the house. She arrived at the door as Millie and Jackson entered. Behind Millie, she asked, "May I sit with you, Millie?"

The surprise on Millie's face was replaced by an enigmatic inscrutability. "Please do, Honey. We have not had preaching here since, well…"

Millie thought a moment. Could she tell without telling? "The strangest thing, Ginny. There's a medallion set in your father's stone. It says it is a presidential medal of merit. I'm thinking Toby did that the last time he was here. You will have to see it."

The crowd gathered, and conversation was muted by curiosity. The bell sent a final call winging down the valley, and when, five minutes later, the door behind the platform opened, there were only a few empty chairs. The worshipers eyed the young man in the well-tailored blue suit as he hung his bowler on the doorknob, and placed his

Bible and notes on the stand.

Toby surveyed the crowd and prayed in opening that the Lord would bless the Word as it went forth, and that God's Spirit would use the truth to convict, to encourage or to strengthen in faith. The focus was still on the speaker and his strong, pleasing voice.

Toby said, "You will notice I scattered hymnals on the chairs. I found that Preacher John had only opened the box, intending to have more singing. He added a piano to help you out. Now, I don't know if it is in tune, and I don't have any idea how to tune it anyway." Laughter rippled through the room. "I can't play it, either. So, if the Lord has prepared anyone here to minister on the ivories, I would be glad if you would step up and play as we sing." He waited a moment. "Well, then, we must sing as…" He stopped as a young woman in blue rose and walked to the piano. She pulled out the bench and turned the instrument slightly to take better advantage of the light from the window. She sat, opened the cover to the keys, and ran a quick arpeggio up the keyboard. Satisfied, she looked to Toby for the number he had chosen.

Toby said, "Preacher John had chosen this for his message, but he died before Sunday. Please turn to the book of Hebrews chapter six, and I will read verses seventeen through twenty. He read, **'Wherein God, willing more abundantly to shew unto the heirs of promise the immutability of his counsel, confirmed it by an oath: that by two immutable things, in which**

it was impossible for God to lie, we might have a strong consolation, who have fled for refuge to lay hold upon the hope set before us: which hope we have as an anchor of the soul, both sure and stedfast, and which entereth into that within the veil; whither the forerunner is for us entered, even Jesus, made an high priest for ever after the order of Melchisedec.'

"Preacher John had underlined the part that relates to believers and the Savior. He had planned to base his sermon on the part that reads, **'who have fled for refuge to lay hold upon the hope set before us.'**

"We want to take note of three things in that phrase. The first is the word *fled*. The second is the word *refuge*. The third is the word *hope*.

"To flee is to run to escape impending danger. It is not just to run from something, but to run to something as well. We flee the hovering wrath of God that broods over every unbeliever. But we flee to the place of safety that God's grace has provided in Christ Jesus. He draws us to that refuge.

"A refuge is a place of security, a place of protection, a shelter in the time of danger. It keeps us safe, and keeps danger at bay.

"Preacher John had added a note of a Scripture that foreshadows the refuge that is ours. It is found back in the book of Exodus. When God was talking to Moses, we read, **'And the LORD said, Behold, there is a place by me, and thou shalt stand upon a rock: and it shall come to pass, while my glory passeth by, that I will put thee in a cleft of the rock, and will cover thee with my hand while I pass by...'"**

Toby looked toward the pianist, and said, "Number three hundred forty-seven, please. I'll give you a nod."

To the crowd, he said, "Preacher John chose this hymn to go with his message. Years ago, I used to sit back there with a little girl who told me this was her father's favorite hymn. I have heard her singing it up by his grave."

A look of astonishment passed over Ginny's face. She thought, "Is that Toby? He's going to preach?"

Toby was saying, "Jesus is that refuge to which we have fled. He is the place of safety from the wrath to come. Let's all sing, *Rock of Ages*."

The confident piano led to even more confident singing:

Rock of Ages, cleft for me,

Let me hide myself in Thee

Let the water and the blood,

From thy wounded side which flowed

Be of sin the double cure,
Save from wrath and make me pure.
Not the labor of my hands
Can fulfill thy law's demands;
Could my zeal no respite know,
Could my tears forever flow,
All for sin could not atone;
Thou must save, and thou alone.

Nothing in my hand I bring
Simply to thy cross I cling;
Naked, come to thee for dress;
Helpless, look to thee for grace;
Foul, I to the fountain fly;
Wash me, Savior, or I die.

While I draw this fleeting breath,
When my eyes shall close in death,
When I rise to worlds unknown,
And behold Thee on Thy throne,

Rock of Ages, cleft for me,

Let me hide myself in thee.

Above the singing of the congregation, Toby heard the clear ringing voice from the piano bench. He smiled. The young lady could both play and sing.

Toby turned again to his Bible. He said, "As we continue Preacher John's theme, we go to the Gospel of John, chapter ten. There, Jesus shows Himself to be our refuge. He is the rock in which we find refuge. He is the one the Exodus passage looked ahead to see, centuries later. In Exodus, God placed his hand over Moses hidden in the cleft of the rock. Look at verses twenty-seven through thirty. Jesus said of believers, who are His flock, His own, **'My sheep hear my voice, and I know them, and they follow me: and I give unto them eternal life; and they shall never perish, neither shall any man pluck them out of my hand. My Father, which gave them me, is greater than all; and no man is able to pluck them out of my Father's hand. I and my Father are one.'** This protection, this relationship, is only afforded to those who are by faith in Christ. For those who do not believe, there is no shelter, no refuge from the wrath to come. Oh, friends, as the apostle Paul says, **'Examine yourselves, whether ye be in the faith; prove your own selves. Know ye not your own selves, how that Jesus Christ is in you, except ye be**

reprobates?' That little girl I knew used to talk with the ground squirrels. They only had one call, given in several tonalities. In this valley, you have heard that call. It always sounds like they are calling, 'Chink-um'! In one tonality, it conveys the urgent message, 'HIDE!' For those outside of Christ, then, that is the message: Chink-um! The Word says the wrath is coming. Moses, without the covering hand of God, would have met disaster. The one outside of Christ, without that covering hand of God, faces the same thing.

"By His grace, God has provided a place of hope, a place of quiet rest for the Savior's flock. They follow where the Shepherd leads, and follow in quiet confidence. They know His voice, and find comfort and encouragement in His presence.

"The word hope in our passage implies a confident expectation that God, who is faithful, will accomplish all that He has promised. His purpose will prevail, for His flock as a whole, and for each individual member. He does all to the praise of His glorious grace."

Toby picked up another paper. "I have a new hymn from Fanny Crosby that is not in the hymnal, but it goes so well with Preacher John's passage that I decided to sing it. If the piano player is able to sight read, that is." He looked across, and caught tears streaming down Ginny's face. As he walked to the piano, he slipped his handkerchief out of his pocket, and handed it to the girl along with the song sheet.

All eyes were on him as he secured his own copy, and closed his Bible while Ginny wiped her eyes. Toby thought, "I've seen her before. I wonder where?"

He stepped forward on the platform and said to Ginny, "Play through it once to find the melody. I'll come in on the second time through." She nodded, and began to play softly, coming to a crescendo when she reached the chorus.

A wonderful Savior is Jesus my Lord,

A wonderful savior to me.

He hideth my soul in the cleft of the rock,

Where rivers of pleasure I see.

He hideth my soul in the cleft of the rock

That shadows a dry, thirsty land.

He hideth my life in the depths of His love,

And covers me there with His hand,

And covers me there with His hand.

A wonderful Savior is Jesus my Lord;

He taketh my burden away.

He holdeth me up, and I shall not be moved;

He giveth me strength as my day.

He hideth my soul in the cleft of the rock

That shadows a dry, thirsty land.

He hideth my life in the depths of His love,

And covers me there with His hand,

And covers me there with His hand.

With numberless blessings each moment He crowns,

And filled with His fullness divine,

I sing in my rapture, "Oh, glory to God

For such a Redeemer as mine!"

He hideth my soul in the cleft of the rock

That shadows a dry, thirsty land.

He hideth my life in the depths of His love,

And covers me there with His hand,

And covers me there with His hand.

When clothed in His brightness, transported I rise

To meet Him in clouds of the sky,

His perfect salvation, His wonderful love,

I'll shout with the millions on high.

He hideth my soul in the cleft of the rock

That shadows a dry, thirsty land.

He hideth my life in the depths of His love,

And covers me there with His hand,

And covers me there with His hand.

Toby's rich baritone massaged the message into the minds of the listeners, and during the days ahead, the Spirit would move the truth from their heads to their hearts. Toby closed with a simple prayer, and the ones who had gathered flocked forward to thank and congratulate him. Would he be there next week? Would the old church see life again, and feed the flock in the valley? He was noncommittal. "I'll pray about that, and see where the Lord leads. Join me in that, will you please?"

Millie lingered in the background, then clung to Toby, her face lined with tears. "Jackson wants to talk with you this afternoon. Pray, Toby. The Lord's working."

Finally, the last worshiper went out the door. Ginny still sat at the piano, dabbing her eyes with Toby's handkerchief. She rose as he walked over, and stood looking at her. "I'm sorry, whatever started the tears. I've seen you somewhere before, Miss. I thank you for stepping up on such short notice, and for tackling a hymn you had never seen. You did well. It must have been of the Lord. But can you help me out? Where have I seen you?"

Blushing, Ginny said, "In the pond. Kiss me, Toby."

"Ginny? Then it was in San Francisco. I did not know you then, until Nobles told me. But I had only glanced at you, and did not see any detail of you. So when you came forward this morning, I had no idea who you were. Come back here." He caught her arm, and led her to the back corner of the church. "Now, where were we? What was that you said a while ago?"

Ginny giggled. "Kiss me, Toby."

He did.

"Kin I love you, Toby"

"I guess, if you want to." He embraced her, and noticed again how soft and cool her lips were. At last, she rested her face against him and sighed. "I asked Jesus to bring us back together."

Toby held her at arm's length. "Ginny, I'm needed here. This little church needs me. Would you serve the Lord here with me? Would you share the house on the hill with me? It is waiting to shelter my wife. We could learn to love each other there. You are not my little girl any more." He held her close, shut his eyes, and sighed. "Honey, He puts in our hearts the desires He delights to fulfill. I asked for the same thing." He kissed the top of her head. Neither lover saw Millie in the doorway.

ABOUT THE AUTHOR

Michael Leamy is a teacher and proclaimer of the Word, among other things. He fancies himself a writer. Kindly indulge him in that delusion. He grew up in a house on a hill above a creek that was too cold and too shallow for swimming. The folds in the hills gave an early sample of Oregon for the setting of the story. In the recesses of his empty head, the author still hears the chink-um of the ground squirrels that occupied tunnels along the edge of the hay field, and sees them standing upright to look about for danger, or climbing to a high point to get a better look. He recalls first hand the isolation in a crowd at a rural school. The characters in this story may resemble real people. If they do, that is a good thing. However, if you see yourself, the writer did not use you as a model.

Michael and his wife Lynda live near the Pacific Ocean, in a house on a hill overlooking a bay in which they do not swim, either with or without swimming clothes. Enjoy the story. Go back and read it again. Then go swimming. With or without.

Made in the USA
Columbia, SC
24 October 2024